WITH KENNEDY

and other stories

WITH KENNEDY

AND OTHER STORIES

James Summerville

Xlibris

This is a work of fiction. Names, characters, places and incidents either are the product of the author's imagination or are used fictitiously, and any resemblance to any actual persons, living or dead, events, or locales is entirely coincidental.

This book was printed in the United States of America.

Xlibris Corporation
1-888-7-XLIBRIS
www.Xlibris.com

Xlibris

CONTENTS

Acknowledgements

The following stories have appeared in magazines and anthologies, usually in slightly different form, and are reprinted here with the author's gratitude to the original publishers.

"Culture Wars," *The Lake Superior Review*, x, no. 1, Summer, 1979 (under the title "The Critic and Mr. Young")
"Getting Airborne," *Old Hickory Review*, xii, no. 1, Spring-Summer, 1981
"The Portrait of a Lady," *Green River Review*, viii, nos. 1 and 2, 1977 (under the title "Legacies")
"Paper Fires," in Douglas Paschall and Alice Swanson, eds., *Homewords; A Book of Tennessee Writers* (Knoxville: The University of Tennessee Press, 1986)
"Taking Possession," *Old Hickory Review*, xiv, no. 2, Fall-Winter, 1982

Books by James Summerville

Educating Black Doctors; A History of Meharry Medical College
Healthy Building For a Better Earth (with Charles A. Howell, III)
Home Place
The Carmack-Cooper Shooting; Tennessee Politics Turns Violent
Southern Epic; Nashville Through 200 Years
With Kennedy and Other Stories

THIS BOOK IS FOR LINDA, WITH LOVE.

PAPER FIRES

Twice a week between October and May, a volunteer from the Community Chest of Nashville drove up the driveway to the back of the house and unloaded a stack of old newspapers. In the coldest weeks of winter, she piled the trunk full, and unloading it took several trips up and down the rotting steps.

A number of times that first autumn, she knocked tentatively at the sprung screen door. When there was no answer, she pushed the papers next to the siding, away from rain. On top of the pile she set a chunk of concrete that she found among the weeds in the yard so that the wind would not scatter the papers.

The neighborhood meat and produce market, when it was sold and changed over to an A&P, stopped delivering to the house, until the manager received a call from the attorney who managed the Albrecht estate. After that the same order was brought and left at the back door, every Monday morning, when customer traffic in the store was the slowest. A generation of sackboys, thinking about inaccessible thighs they had glimpsed in the housewares aisle, trundled the loads onto the listing porch while the radio rattled in the cab of the truck.

One summer the city sent a notice that cited the ordinance against keeping an unkempt lot. The rusted mailbox overflowed with department store circulars and newsletters from the local Congressman, but since the city's letter was sent first class, the postman slipped it between the peeling door and the jamb.

After dark, Leisl Albrecht, leaning on her cane, trudged through the hallway. The passage was bare except for a rock that someone had thrown through a sidelight, the glistening trail of glass, and the dust that her slippers raised. The door opened on the night air; the envelope clattered to the floor. Bending, she picked it up and was gone again, tugging the bolt shut behind her.

Some weeks after the order to clean up the property came, a car with official plates turned into the drive, the frothy heads of the Queen Anne's Lace thumping against its grill. For several minutes it sat with the motor running. Then it backed slowly out into the traffic, which was beginning to swell with evening rush hour. No more notices came, and in the third week of October, when the first cold blew across the city, the old woman used the notice to kindle her first paper fire.

Sometimes the wind, ringing and tapping the windows in their frames, roused her in her sleep. Then she would dream, until the chill brought her fully awake, that the sound was Father's boots on the stairway to the rooms where they had lived when they first came to the city.

Every year until the war began, a new pair arrived from Father's cobbler in the town not far from the Ruhr, where Leisl had been born. The hard heels, fixed by fine, thin nails, shook the steps as Papa climbed, crossed the landing, and flung open the door.

Cast by the hallway lamp behind him, his shadow covered Leisl. In an undertow not to be resisted, he gathered her up from among her alphabet blocks. Her face was pressed against his starch collar, and she heard his voice through the bones of her head.

"My little girl, she has been good?"

"Yes, Papa."

"Mama will not tell me that she has disobeyed?"

"No, Papa."

"She has learned the letters on the blocks that I gave to her?"

"Of course, Papa."

When she grew too tall to be lifted into his arms, she learned to curtsy. In time, he offered her his cheek to kiss, with its day's growth of sharp whiskers. His questions scarcely changed in form as the years passed, and her answers remained as unvarying as a nun's.

There had been no physician in the immigrant community

until they arrived in 1910. Dr. Albrecht was honored with a banquet in the millwrights' hall.

In three years his success purchased Mama a piano. One day at lunchtime he brought home some sheets of music bundled tightly in a roll. Sweeping his hand above the keyboard, he gathered up the scores by Wagner and Liszt and set out the new pieces. One the cover of one of them, a young man and woman rowed on a moon-streaked lake. The tinny notes, when he played them on the ivory, hung light and cool in the midday air.

For Leisl Mama was able to buy mail-order dresses from New York. The childhood frocks brought across the ocean she packed away in a leather-strapped trunk. The bright new things she lay in the deep, scented drawers of the bureau.

On Sunday as they walked toward the buggy after church, the wife of Hoefner, the mercantilist, stopped Mama and asked her her reasons for never appearing in their store. "Fine goods from home we have," Frau Hoefner said, "and not dear."

Mama replied politely, acknowledging the old ties. But alone later with her daughter, she said that it was strictly necessary for Leisl to present herself as the other girls did. When the first day of school was over, she asked about the dresses and blouses and shoes that Leisl's classmates wore, and only then about the beginning lesson in sums. Under the green lamp they turned through the New York catalog. "Like this?" Mama asked. "Were they dressed as this one is?"

A dozen years later, after they moved to the never-finished house on the edge of town, after the dinner party that was never held—all Leisl's clothes that Mama had bought by mail were taken from the bureau and thrust deep into the old trunk in the attic. Its straps were cinched tightly shut.

Parts of the roof, when it began to give way, lay open to the air for years, and in the winter the frost drew heat upward from Leisl Albrecht's paper fires. Once a starling fluttered through one of the gaps in a mindless search for food and, unable to find its way out again, screeched itself to exhaustion and died. The bones and the dust moiling around them lay next to the rusting trunk.

The house was the great boon from Father's practice. In the spring of 1914 he bought the house in Belmont Heights and commissioned the builders to begin.

To move from the old community was daring. But the city's future, Papa declared to Leisl and Mama, lay along the roads, being laid now past the towers of the Vanderbilt University and on to the edge of the farms on the old battlefields of the Civil War.

"You will like the house, little one, I am sure of it," Papa said to Leisl as the buggy raised the hot dust from the road and twirled it behind them. From beneath the canopy's quivering fringe, and stared at the university's massive Main Building. It came into view each time there was a space between the maples, covered with amber dust.

The unfinished house in the rude suburb was quite acceptable to Leisl once she discovered she would be able to see the Main Building's parapets from the window of her room.

Young women not much older than she now matriculated at the college. Some of them, she had heard, even went into town unchaperoned. She glimpsed one of them, not long after they moved to the new house that summer. "Co-eds," they were called. She wondered how it would feel to wear her hair according to the co-ed fashion.

In the morning Leisl sat at her dressing table, pulling a brush through its heat-tangled length and pausing now and then to rest her hands on the glass top.

At every quarter hour the couple who lived in the cupola of the clock on the mantle took a turn around their unvarying path. She looked up to watch them until they disappeared behind the tiny wooden doors. Then the single tone faded, the hammers and wheels sank into silence, and the ticking made the only sound in the vast room.

It made her giddy to contemplate the patterns and contrivances that were deliberately made to seem matters of choice. Where was the caprice in the marriages that at the moment of the figurines' stroll sank into speechlessness on the other side of town? And the errors posted by countless clerks in the last hurried transactions of the day that could multiply into ruin. And where was the play of life in the artifice and will of others, by whom she had been raised? How was she different from the objects in the house?

Her father's purposes in building the new house were scarcely corrupt, she knew. Through the house, life was revealed not to have been turns blindly taken but an orderly progress, begun with the passage to America.

Nonetheless, when she could she would divest herself of its leaden weight. She was willing to have nothing at all if she could have pure, clear discernment about life. She longed for perfect clarity and understanding, devoid of things and undiluted by certainties. Such a house as this hid all private disquiet; such safety stopped life.

As she rose from the dressing table and walked to the window to see the towers of the college in the falling sun, the hammering on the west lawn ceased. Leisl watched as the Negroes dropped their tools into a cloth satchel and flung it onto a worm-gnawed buckboard. Roused from sleep, the mule flinched and shimmied as the men climbed onto the seat. The animal turned a wide, lazy circle and sauntered off, the trio bobbing on the spavined springs.

Mama postponed the paying of calls while their new neighbors were away at Monteagle or Beersheeba Springs for the hottest days of summer. One evening in September, at dinner, she mentioned her felt obligations. Papa gazed at the ceiling high above.

"For an evening." he said. "All of them we will invite. It will not be necessary, absolutely, that everything be finished first."

It required many tasks, nonetheless, to ready the house for guests. Mama and Leisl dipped their table linens in the foul-smelling starch and shaped each one with their hands. They raised the new floors to a high gloss. The face of the grandfather's clock was hidden behind the sheen they put on its convex face. The air of the house smelled of the rosewood polish that Leisl applied to the banister of the stairs.

Mama wrote the invitations by hand and from house to house in the neighborhood they halted the buggy, on an afternoon when the thunderheads were piled high in the sky The reins grew slick in Leisl's palms.

At each gate Mama took an envelope and, lifting her hem out of the burning dust of the road, strode to the door.

A house servant curtsied and took the proffered envelope, studying the queerly formed letters. Over the sound of insects that dipped against the blooming vines, Mama introduced herself as Mrs. Herr Doctor Albrecht and made her practiced speech. Then smiling at the blank face, she turned to the steps, her mesh purse swinging from her wrist. In the cool, dim interior, the servant shut the door softly, against the heat.

Papa helped with the preparations on the day of the dinner party. While Leisl and Mama broke open the cabbages and sliced the potatoes for dumplings, he pounded the schnitzel into tenderness with the blunt face of a cleaver.

It was not yet four o'clock when he declared that it was time for the table to be set. Carrying the felt-lined box, Mama paused at each place while Leisl took out spoons, forks, cutlery. They stood the napkins stiff as sentries and, opposite each, set down a sparkling goblet.

Following Mama as she set the plates, Leisl aligned each glass so that from the head of the table where Papa would sit the points of light that sparkled from them inscribed a rigid but stellar line.

It was, of course, a trick. The long table required the slightest asymmetry from glass to glass if to Papa's perspective they were to appear perfectly ordered. Without glancing to the side, Leisl went and stood at his place and shutting her eyes she let go the knowledge that the order was an allusion; and when she opened them again she saw the table as Papa would.

When in the evening would come his vision for her, the first glimmer that she ought to attend the university? Amid the tableaux in front of her, she placed herself as Papa would see her. She imagined the professor of chemistry as, halfway to his mustache, he halted his napkin to reflect on the remark that Leisl had just made. And there was the Latinist who would select a dried fruit that Leisl had offered, chewing it gravely while he pondered her respectful query. For the first time Papa would see her in the setting where she belonged. He would smile thinly and nod slightly to himself at the next confirming bestowal from the new world, that his daughter should become a "co-ed."

She stood over the last simmering kettle while her parents went upstairs to dress. In her turn, in the last afternoon light from her window, she dried her hair. The maples, mountainous and stolid in the motionless air, waited for a breeze to sift the light of the shortening days through them. Then at her mirror she drew the tiny compact from the drawer where she had concealed it since the secret purchase.

When she came down to the parlor, Papa was turning the pages of the new *Collier's*, and Mama had taken up her needlepoint. For the cool of the evening she had opened the curtains.

Between the house and the city a mile away, the haze was deepening. In the slate-gray air the fireflies made their gentle waves. Through the trees the streetlights in town flickered. The spires of the churches that sunlight seemed to diffuse into the hot metallic sky receded into their simplest lines and blocks and angles. Above the lavender clouds in the west the first star appeared, faint and red.

Soon, at any moment, cooling dust in the road would fly from beneath shunting hooves, and the horses, whinnying in their traces and shaking sweat from themselves, would draw up before the gate. A petticoat would rasp faintly on the boards of the porch and then would come the rap, rap, rap of the knuckles from which the traces of chalk had been scrubbed or the scent of money washed over by cologne.

As daylight seeped out the foyer, the hands of the clock emerged to view. The light of the moon rising over the hills to the east reached the heights of the new house and the tower that vaulted over the university. Beyond the two, the pasture lands and fields and old, bloodied wilderness deepened into darkness.

A rain crow called out of some dark place, and the clock struck eight notes. On her stool by the cupboard, Leisl marked time with her heel and tool as on the table the cooling broth began to leaven.

Papa had sheared slices from the cheese with a paring knife. For a long time she watched the faintly darkening edges, humming a song that Papa had favored them with one noon at the piano. Then she reached across to the silver tray and pinched a morsel from the yellow mound. Slowly she bit into it and, listening for the hooves, chewed quietly. She was eating a third morsel when the pure crystal tone of the half hour rang through the house. The taste turned sharp and sour on her tongue.

She raised her eyes over the table, where all things she had arrayed there had been rising toward some new composition. After the dinner party, these objects and the house were to belong to the past, and seen by the light of the future in the shadow of the tower that rose above Belmont Heights.

In the silence that followed the chime, each one began to regain its relentless turn proportion. From the bosom of the creamer a rivulet of water rolled, dropped, and spread on the stiff tablecloth.

No dreamed-of thought, no thought-of thought had prepared her for such refusal as this. A cup with a gilt rim answered her unfocused stare.

No one? she thought. *No one at all?*

That meant, of course, that the dreamers would walk and talk without her on the cobblestone walks under the magnolias. Behind garret windows they would compose their books, written against time. If any of it was of any use in clearing new spaces to the west, she was not now likely to learn. All that was possible to foresee was that the blows of the hammers wielded by the laborers would carry the city on beyond them. As the crickets chirped in the thistles, the mule was even now carrying the workmen on their ramshackle buckboard down into the bottoms of the old town. There it would stand until after midnight, the mule sleeping a blind dumb sleep as the music blared from a dim dance parlor.

Father stood in the doorway of the dining room. He had set his heavy jaw, and his face was the color of one who had walked a long distance on a cold day.

For the first time since they had come to America, he spoke in the language that Mama had screamed when the girl was born. She might clear the table, he said. Then she was to wash her face.

At the gate at daylight Papa met the workmen. There would be no need, after all, to hang the gutters on the eaves, he told them, and he paid them for the work they had done through the day before on the gazebo. Before the end of September, the relentless grass had sprung up in the unfinished well of it.

The autumn was unusually wet, and the water pouring in sheets from the roof of the house faintly streaked the new wood and carved shallow trenches in the ground. The multicolored sand washed from the shingles of the roof and collected there. That winter puddles froze and began to push against the foundation.

Ten years passed before the first tiny cracks appeared in the piers that supported the roof line. By that time a score more new houses were being raised along the road from the city, which passed the Vanderbilt and traveled south. A councilman lived on this crowding length, nearest the cottages of the machinists and clerks. Further out, a vice president of the Louisville and Nashville raised a confection of a house and brought small ponies to roam on the vast front yard.

The same year that the crest of Dr. Albrecht's house toppled into the untended side yard, the chancellor of the university moved into the neighborhood. When he read the news in the social columns of the *Banner*, Papa laughed out loud, behind the door that was shut against his waiting room. He kept his office in the old precinct, where most of his countrymen had lived before they changed their names, or lost them as the children of their children moved out into the town. In time he sold his horses and bought a

Model T, which he drove two miles each day, to his office and home again. They ceased to attend church, reading aloud to each other from the Bible on Sunday morning instead.

The interior of the house remained comfortable as the thorns overtook the porch. By 1938 it became necessary to close the part of the second floor where plaster had begun to sag.

Father died in his bed on the eve of the Second World War. The letter signed by his neighbors asking him to attend to his property for the good of the community marked his place in the poems of Heinrich Heine, which lay on the bedside table. The estate would be adequate, the lawyer promised Mama and Leisl, and he promised to see to whatever they needed.

Mama grew old, busying herself steaming labels from empty jars or nodding to sleep in her rocker. The round face that Father had once thought beautiful was no more, as gaps appeared among her teeth. Sometimes she would forget what year it was.

One day Leisl hurried into the room when she heard her mother quietly murmuring. Pointing to an empty chair by the draughty window, the old woman introduced her daughter to her aunt, who had died in an epidemic when Mama and she were young girls. In her last illness she talked senselessly about the son she had wanted to bear.

The goods that Leisl cared to save she pushed and pulled, one at a time, into the middle room farthest from the elements. Fall, the first after her mother's death, was coming in earnest. The frost had already wrinkled the fluted flowers of the creeper vines along the windowsill. The horn blasts of the train that left the city at dawn carried through the molting trees. Cold weather had come when the relief volunteer called for the first time with the trunk full of newspapers.

They might have brought Leisl Albrecht the war news, but she did not read them before she twisted them into logs and kindled them with loose pages saved by.

In the winter the charity woman piled the papers as high as the hem of her coat. One a visit one February, when the ice crunched under her tires in the driveway, she came twice with new loads to find that the rock on the top of the pile had not been moved. A yellow and red comic page was flattened over it by the wind.

Without unloading the car, she drove to the gas station in the next block and telephoned the attorney. By the time he arrive it was the nameless hour of late afternoon. The sun made bright flecks in the dirty snow along the shoulders of Belmont Boulevard. He told the dispatcher at the general hospital that there would be no need for the lights or the siren.

The ambulance nonetheless came blaring down the street, twisting in and out of traffic, and bounced, blaring and flashing, up the rutted driveway. The two attendants rolled the stretcher to the front door and locked the wheels. On the return trip they stepped carefully as the boards sagged under their feet and the awful weight under the sheets swung between them.

THEIRS TO CLAIM

Bully Hickerson was starting the last section of the culvert to the holding pond when his backhoe struck the iron box holding the gold of the Confederate States of America.

The cleats clanged, the chassis shuddered, and the exhaust pipe spewed brown smoke. Hot damn, Bully muttered, peering into the scarred ground. If this was another blame Indian grave, he knew, they'd have to stop work and call the state people.

He slapped the gear knob, got down, grabbed a shovel and scrapped the dirt from the lid of the box. The clasps were rusty, and when he struck the lock with the side of his blade, it dropped off. The hinges creaked, and inside were what looked like dirty yellow bricks. Mud had rimed them where water had got in.

Moving the box was no job for a man just before retirement, Bully thought. He called over a couple of the summer college boys, and they dug and pulled and finally wrenched it out of the dirt and dragged it over to the side and sat it among the construction debris of pallets, metal sheathings, and bundling wire.

Richlande was past due on its notes, and the word was on the street that the loan had gone bad. But they'd gotten zoning for another phase, 700 more apartment units, and Bully figured the boss would be riding his crew even worse than usual.

An hour later Chip himself stepped out of a Land Rover driven by the councilman for the area. They'd had to hold the usual public hearings to get the extra units, and there an old woman had pressed on him a picture of General John Calvin Trescott, C.S.A., and a yellow newspaper clipping about how he'd spirited Jefferson Davis out of Richmond with whatever was left of his government that they could carry in a buckboard.

Chip had handed the clipping to the p.r. firm handling the sales kit. They recommended calling the upper-end home sites Richlande, Trescott's old plantation. The developer promised neighbors to control the runoff from the parking lots, and the councilman said that was good enough for him and put through the new zoning. Chip named the streets he platted across the Trescott farm Adelaide Place and Sydney Boulevard, because he was sleeping with a pert Australian girl, a paralegal at the firm that handled the title work.

This Friday night, with the market's closing bell rung, he and Felicity were planning to drive out beyond the city to a party in a backyard that led down past a satellite dish to a purling creek where nothing lived any longer. It was still a green, good place where they could see the night sky, and the stars in constellations, that once had names, shined like so much money in a private vault above the world.

Bully showed Chip the culvert work they'd done that week and the little there was to finish. Did he want them to put in the overtime? And what about the old box, should he call the archaeology office?

Chip was anxious to pick up his girl. "No, I want you all grading for those apartment footings next week. So finish up over here today.

"And, Bully," he said, pointing to the gold. "Looks to me like just some old foundation stone. We don't have time to waste. Just get shut of it."

When they quit for dark, Bully went and got his pickup, drove back to the job site, and loaded the old bricks out of the chest and into the bed. The iron box was left for a subcontractor that hauled away building junk and resold it for government work.

Bully and Mariam had brought their place with a 30-year FHA loan. When Baby Laura arrived they built a room for her. She was engaged now to Michael, a fellow scriptwriter at the advertising firm where she worked, and the room was Mariam's mother, confined to bed with rheumatoid arthritis. Bully's days in the hot sun paid for her pain medication and cable t.v.

In the garage sat Laura's old aquarium, gathering dust, and his mother-in-law's folded walker. Hickerson stacked the bricks one by one under his carpenter's bench.

Mariam Hickerson's mother died two months before the bank foreclosed on Richlande. All that summer weeds grew along Sydney Boulevard, then a health care corporation took over the mortgage. Following his retirement, Mariam begged her husband to put her in a flowerbed under the living room window. He laid the old bricks at an angle to each other and set bare rose bushes in the raised ground.

They were in bloom in May when the bride and groom came back to Laura's home to cut the cake. Her high school classmates waited three deep at the door to hug her and shake her new husband's hand. The scent of perfumed candles wafted out the church door as the happy couple hurried through the misting rain to their waiting carriage. The horse and driver set out by the side streets, drops plashing against the leather roof. Michael's boutonniere was smashed, and Laura's face grew flush in the minutes that passed. They released each other as the clip clopping hooves drew them up before the Hickerson home.

Long ago, the men had come back from the war and taken up plowing, leaning into the harness and brace for fifty and sixty years, with seldom a dance, a game, a feast. Now, young again, a company of them stood at attention side by side along the walk, in silver gray light. As Laura stepped down from the carriage, they raised a canopy of gleaming sabers under which the bride and her husband rushed, laughing, toward the waiting friends.

GETTING AIRBORNE

It had been Hurwitz's idea to give the Cultural Hero medal, of course. Only an ingenue, a political naïf could have come up with it, and that's exactly what he was, fresh out of the divinity school of a famous university in New Haven, whose name you've probably heard.

The Mayor had been thinking about writing a book called *A Christian in Politics*, and that's why he'd hired Hurwitz, to sort of help him get his thoughts together. "I always did feel like I had a book in me," was the way the Mayor put it.

"You always wanted to be governor of the damn state, too," I reminded him. "Right now, you wouldn't even carry half a dozen precincts in this city. Did you see what the Black Voters Council is saying—I'm quoting Tom Crome now—'His Honor done done it to us again.'"

"T.C. must practice that hokey jive talk while he shaves every day," the Mayor said.

I assured him that Crome used it with big accounts at his bank, sprinkled it through the editorials of his community tabloid, *Black Times*, and was even known to lapse into it when he preached at Calvary Union Church on Sunday mornings. Then I sprang on him Hurwitz's memo about the Cultural Hero medal.

" 'Fore God," he said when he had read it. "I wished I was out on number one fairway."

"You remember T. Wilson Fahrquar? Wrote this book after he retired as president of Poston College? What we'd do is, you'd present the first Cultural Hero medal to his widow, at a ceremony in his honor."

The boss just sighed in a pathetic sort of way and slumped

back in his swivel chair. "You believe that story they always tell, about old Poston giving a million dollars to start a college for former slaves? Just because a black man had helped him when he got lost in a swamp as a boy?"

I shrugged and looked down at the carpet.

"Okay, okay," he said. "We'll do it. Just make sure in the speech that I sound like I've regard Fahrquar's book as one of the immortal works of Western man."

I told him that if he could ever mask his sense of the ridiculous he might get somewhere in politics. I expected a volume of the city code to slam between my shoulders as I left the office.

In his first draft Hurwitz faulted the book from the title page ("*Getting Airborne* is an ill-chosen metaphor for the history of a college") to certain lapses in the footnotes. "The Mayor is not speaking before the faculty union," I wrote back. "Just get some quotes—'brotherhood of man' stuff—and the basic outline."

For the ceremony I rented a semi, and managed to scout up a country-western singer and a soul food street vendor, too. We parked the truck in front of city hall, and toward the end of the lunch hour the guitar had drawn a crowd. On cue I sent the Mayor bounding down the steps, into the upturned lens of a "live action" camera.

We didn't want to keep Mrs. Fahrquar out under the sun too long, and His Honor was inclined to perspire heavily. So he simply read Hurwitz's insincere little speech about the late educator and his book and put the first Cultural Hero medal into Mrs. Fahrquar's etched and yellow hands. Only then, with the cameras clicking at her, did he draw his handkerchief across his forehead.

Of awards there was no end. Three times a week, on the average, the Mayor presented a certificate, a plaque, a ribbon, and as many came his way. The most cynical view of it was that prizes called attention to the giver. Awards went, after all, to those who got awards.

If our motives in honoring Fahrquar of Poston were not exactly pure, they were also not hard to rationalize: We needed the Black

Voters Council if my boss was going to be elected governor. A certain insouciance, a casual air might be fine for frustrated scholars like Hurwitz, whom the Mayor seemed to attract. But the rest of us developed a passion for detail. Such single-mindedness was the only way of being, in politics. There were always the klieg lights and the relentless cassette tape that caught every word. One mistake and one's whole strategy toward higher things would all come tumbling down.

I didn't often wonder what the boss would say if he had known that I had been for several years the lover of Tom Crome's wife.

"You're fired!" for starters. He wouldn't even have taken into consideration the fact that he'd been responsible for its happening.

Anyone as steeped in compromise as I was was bound to be forever seeking one perfect thing. For me it was Clarissa's flawless legs. When I first glimpsed them, and her, she was only 23, and unmarried. In her playing dress, she was waiting by the gate to the municipal tennis courts while the attendant made a call to see whether he should admit her.

In the Deep South it was Freedom Summer. Locally, Clarissa had a growing reputation as a poet and a record of arrests for being black and where she wasn't wanted.

I was a junior member of the Mayor's staff then, and he had decided to send me over to observe her attempt to integrate the courts, in case of trouble. I was disguised as a player, a ruse no one could possibly have believed.

Clarissa was not about to be taken off to jail that day. The attendant might not have recognized her partner, but I did. Just by being Somebody Somebody, III, he had earned a host of exemptions from life, one of which was freedom from unwanted attention. There would be no story and no pictures since, as his father would explain to the city editor, it was only a young man's test of his elder's taboos before finding them wise and useful.

The park authorities didn't turn the lights on as it grew late.

But the gesture was probably lost on Clarissa, as she and her partner fell to argue about what had been proven and by whom.

"—And don't twirl the racket on the concrete, Jonathan, or I'll have to restring it," she said. I could hear only the muttering he made in reply. Clarissa looked vastly superior, and I had the feeling that he was invisible to her before he marched off the court.

"Hey," she called to me. "You been stood up?"

I said that it was beginning to look that way.

"I believe we could get in a game before it gets too dark," she said, and saw my hesitation. "I don't think the photographer will be back."

"It's not that," I said too quickly. "I'm just not in your class-"

She started to laugh.

"I mean, as a player. My friend was going to give me lesson number one. But, uh, he's in the market, and I guess he had to meet a client."

One thing I'd already learned in politics: if you wanted a lie to be believed, put in lots of specifics and details.

"Okay, then," she said. "We can get in Lesson Number One."

A half hour later she allowed that I wasn't what you could call a natural.

By that time it was too dark to see, or be seen, so I offered her a ride home. I pretended to miss turns and she pretended not to notice, reaching across the seat to turn up the volume when The Supremes came on.

"Don't you just love it?" she said. Eventually I was to hear her ask the same imperious question about the *Village Voice*, a soda shop in the old downtown, Tom Wolfe's latest novel, and the city's Union Station, abandoned now.

We repaired to the stone house where she lived, through which the warps and woofs of the zeitgeist blew. The walls were hung with tintypes, a poster of a rock star, and a photo of herself posed with Chubby Checker. In various corners she had set clay pots with withered stalks, an astrolabe, a drawing board, and shelves made of brick and glass. Mobiles hung from the ceiling, and spices, pastas, cafes spilled from kitchen cabinets. A baby grand piano filled the sunroom, and there were found objects scattered all over: driftwood, polychrome rocks, a length from a frieze depicting children at play. Clarissa had placed a stopwatch on one of the flying heels.

It came out, of course, whom I worked for. Clarissa giggled and spilled some wine on her skirt before she could set down her glass.

"Do I detect a hint of disappointment?" I asked.

She dabbed at the spot with a napkin. "No," she said. "That means you're something less than totally innocent," doesn't it?"

I smiled, sipped, hesitated under her sweet, relentless gaze. Finally I set my glass beside hers. Half emptied, they betrayed our haste.

In public she could be hard as nails and so proved perfect for the local news that slipped into entertainment and out again. A thunderstorm fell the afternoon of the first march for peace in Viet Nam, and she was soaked. They happened to turn the camera on her just as she was lifting the hem of her skirt to step over a gutter awash.

"You were great," I told her.

Cross, she muttered. "I was not 'great'; I was soaking wet."

I said what I had meant, "You were beautiful."

That made her positively furious. "I thought you watched the news, man! Your boss order that rain in here? No? Well he didn't exactly pray for it to stop, either, did he?"

I told her to let us know in advance next time, and we'd get a man on it.

"Okay," she said. "It's time." It was her usual plea with me when she was exasperated. I knew then to stop the joking, to come across.

It was one of her many retorts to my dim imagination. In politics, one determined never to be startled or amazed since that could mean one was uninformed. Clarissa insisted that surprise become the object of our lives.

The democratic nighttime was, for years, the only part of the day when we could be abroad together. The city belonged to Clarissa then, even more than in the hours when she wrote her poems about it. She knew a foreman who'd let us visit his blackboard factory at midnight, "the darkest place there is," she said. She knew the dawn tenants of the wharf, and sometimes she appeared still in her evening clothes at the farmers' market just as they were unloading the produce for Saturday's sale. Solitary walkers were drawn to her, and automat philosophers, and all sorts of fey, marginal people who nurtured their esthetics in garret rooms. And she found a personal meaning in the ballads of the day about children of darkness and the novels from peripatetic boys and girls who roamed the land.

Eventually, of course, she did grip down fast in one place.

One midnight our footsteps through an alleyway fell in syncopation to a saxophone shimmering from a basement dive, and I felt her slip behind me in the darkness.

"Clarissa?" I said softly.

A half minute passed while the trumpeter teased the crowd.

"Darling?"

Still she didn't answer.

Then she stepped forward, grasping one of my elbows and the other shoulder. With her lead we were at the curb in the streetlight. A gold necklace I'd once given her lay pale against her smooth brown neck that she tilted up to show me the open field of her face.

"Dark lady," I said.

She let her hands fall to mine. Her fingertips raised little tracks of fire.

It proved to be enough that I merely accepted her going forward into her black past. After all, she only acquired a reference and reserved a point upon which to stand. That was no more than virtually everyone does in selecting some partial view, raising it to a whole, and promoting one's investment therein.

Dutifully I read in proof the scholarly article she wrote on

Gullah, and I tottered on a stepladder to hang in the stone house portraits of forgotten race heroes.

When she was elected to Congress the first time, Tom Crome delivered nine precincts for her. Their names were already linked by local gossip when their photograph appeared in back to back numbers of *Ebony* and *Jet*.

She was not accustomed to being on the defensive with me, and she was awkward about it. "I made him no bargain. For the votes, I mean."

"Then I guess it was made in heaven," I said, imagining as usual that the very air crackled with my irony.

Clarissa just reached up an loosened my tie. "Well, not exactly in heaven, I don't think. It was just love, see. Down-to-earth. Basic. Ordinary." And she added, "Hey, Mr. High-and-Mighty. It's time."

She went on loving everything she saw, and simply grew bolder along with the age. She would breeze right past my desk, straight into the Mayor's office. They'd salute each other with the clenched fist (he required some instruction from her to make his convincing) and speculate jovially about the degree of my commitment to the revolution. The boss insisted that it was steadfast, while Clarissa was more than a little dubious.

Our dreamspace was narrowed to the wallpapered rooms in the great Victorian block where I rented. I sometimes didn't even bother to draw the curtains by way of participating in the general shamelessness. Afterwards I would lie listening, as Clarissa's bare feet skittered across the carpet to her hastily cast-off shoes, then to the door and some new facet of her destiny. No one disputes that a man lives and dies alone, but that he make love alone is not generally known.

A few days after we awarded the first Cultural Hero medal, a copy of the newspaper serial that T. Wilson Fahrquar had plagiarized to write his book arrived in the mail, bearing no return address. I was bent over a map of the newest annexation area, when Hurwitz slid the microfilm copies onto the plain beyond the city.

The story began "One day in 1826, fourteen year old Frederick Poston became lost in a swamp. . . ." Fahrquar's cheap, self-published book I had to retrieve from underneath some planning studies. On page one, it mimed along: "One day in 1826, fourteen year old Frederick Poston. . . ." I let the cardboard cover flutter to a close.

So it wasn't necessarily me who shooed away the anointing doves. Even if I had never loved Clarissa, the boss might have done just what he did, retired to Florida after his term and bought a bait and tackle shop with the royalties from *A Christian in Politics*. As for T.C., I doubt if he ever knew that the closest utterances I ever made to poetry, and of a fashionable Neolithic kind, were in his wife's exquisite, unstinting embrace.

You couldn't be sure, though. From the day we presented the Cultural Hero medal, he always greeted me with "Hey, brother! What's happening?" I wondered if it was the peculiar fraternity one felt for a cuckold or the easy intimacy you can take with a fool.

In the aftermath of the award, he summoned up all his indignation and uttered the most devastating charge he could think of: "Amateurs!" began *Black Times'* leading editorial the next week. Hurwitz clipped it, circled the word, and passed it along with a note pointing out that it came from the Latin "amare"—"to love."

Every day produced its unsent letters, unshared memoranda, speeches never heard, and notes that strained after an order of march. In the city's daily archive, there were also heaps of commercial paper, rolls of cash register tape, files, and claims, and canceled checks kept for a quarter of century, then tossed out two days before a notice of audit arrives. There were fragments of poems and careless letters of love. And there were stalks of bouquets that I had imagined thrusting into welcoming hands. As often as not I carried them home to my high-ceilinged rooms, even if they did not match the wallpaper.

Gathered and preserved with a shaping intelligence, it all would have been our history, too, at least as much as any misbegotten book. Instead it was carried down to the airport landfill in public works' huge blue trucks and spread by a tractor blade over the previous day's contribution.

When the first 747 lifted off the following winter on its maiden flight from the city, five hundred lives rode on this vast impacted evidence of dreams.

That same day I got a postcard from Hurwitz. He had joined the boss in his shop near Key West, which they opened, or didn't, pretty much as they pleased.

On sunny days, he wrote, they plunged the prow of the Mayor's cruiser into the waves, then weighed anchor and slept on the deck, while the little toothpick boat turned slowly round and round on the limitless diamond sea.

LUCY'S STORY

When Mama called for Andrew to help her empty the chinapress so that she could sweep behind it, Byron slipped into the parlor to read the letter again.

The double doors of the middle room had been thrown open and the windows raised in their sashes. A breeze was carrying out into the yard the lingering smells of a closed house in winter. Scents from Christmas spices were routed, and odors of polish rose from the trim of the clock on the mantle, the banisters of the stairs. On the porcelain cabinet by her recliner, Grandmother Lucy's medicines gave up sharp, queer smells from about their cork stoppers.

Byron did not greet the old lady, but he did speak to the Persian cat, John Nance, lying in the sun on the windowsill. John Nance, unlike his namesake, seldom had much to say. He was an old cat, nearly as old in feline years as Grandmother Lucy was in human ones. But she, who was 97, was still the quieter of the two. She had not spoken one word in nearly ten years.

In the sunlit parlor, Mama had fixed the window shades facing the road at exactly the same height, as she did every morning of the world. "I want everybody who goes by to know that this house is doing its part to keep up standards," she said. Three high-backed chairs sat as straight as boarding school girls. The doily on the Victoria fell flush with its sides. On the stairstep shelves above, three ceramic ballerinas with perpetual smiles performed their pirouettes. The pendulum of the clock made the only motion in the room.

On the table by the sofa sat a coal oil lamp that Mama kept filled in the event that one of Hitler's buzz bombs reached the power station. The letter was just inside the drawer. Byron took the creased sheets of notebook paper out of the envelope and read:

> Dear sister Rose and boys,
>
> I am in hopes that this finds you all well and enjoying beautiful spring weather, although here in Detroit it is still chilly.
>
> There is ice in the lake yet, and the children at the Catholic school down the street are still skating in the park. The sisters watch them with hands tucked inside those droopy sleeves. I don't know what they could do if the ice broke, they couldn't anymore swim in them habits than anything.
>
> You remember I told you that Jerry's company had got a contract from the War Department to build airplane parts at the plant down close to New Orleans.
>
> Well they are offering to pay the expenses of welders that wants to move down there and Jerry has decided that we could make a better living where things are not so high as they are here. Plus the fact that we have always wanted to come back south.
>
> We are going to go down on the 18th of this month for him to start in work, and since we will be coming through we thought we could stop by and visit with you all. The boys, you know, have never seen their cousin Eleanor, she is going on 17—

From the back of the house came the sound of a china plate shattering on the linoleum floor, followed by Mama's wail, "Oh, Andrew!" then the slamming of the screen door. Quickly Byron folded the letter, replaced it in the drawer, and stepped to the window. Andrew was walking through the sunlight kicking at tufts of grass. His head was bent, and his hands hung in his pockets like weights.

"All that boy's good for is reading books," Byron thought. "He hasn't got a bit of common sense. If the war goes on long enough and we have to go, he won't know which end is up. At least I'll be able to shoot a gun and to find my way if I get separated from my outfit. Mama said Grandpa Thompson sometimes pretended like he was lost and got Yankee patrols to follow him right into his own camp."

Byron was thick in stature, like peach gum. His fingers could round on nothing larger than a baseball, but his shoulders applied against a dead tree could sometimes bring it down.

Pudgy as a child, waddling as a toddler, he had, a few years earlier clipped a coupon and sent away for a book about body-building, then taken to the woods to practice the exercises that produced the power in his arms.

Only recently his mother allowed him to have a .22 on condition that Mr. Monroe who sold it to her at the hardware store agree to come out on the afternoon he closed early and teach Byron how to hit tin cans. Ever since, he moved through the woods with ease. He seemed to take on its colors. He was only sometimes uneasy in the house now, as when he had to sit in the parlor for company's sake. Other times, whenever he could, he wore the cor-duroy pants and flannel shirt that smelled of Mama's cheap, strong laundry powders.

He started back toward the kitchen where his mother was, to help her with getting ready for their company. In Grandmother Lucy's room the ticking of the clock seemed even louder than it had in the parlor.

"I hope Eleanor's pretty," he thought. "I bet she'd even like to shoot my rifle."

The crash awakened Lucy from her dozing. Slowly she blinked her leaden eyelids, then gathered a tiny pool of spit from the cor-ner of her mouth.

"Now Rose will begin to cry," she thought. It was true. From the kitchen came the sound of whimpering.

"I do not mind so much that she must tell every visitor to this house her stories about the china and point out the serving plate I

34   JAMES SUMMERVILLE

once sat before the Governor. But piece by piece the service is bound to be lost, and she ought not to trouble herself about it.

"It's true, of course—the Governor frequently took dinner with her father and me. A duller, cruder man it would be hard to imagine. He always tucked his napkin into his collar and draped it across the front of his Prince Albert coat. But then he ignored it throughout the meal, while gravy dribbled down his chin. He was so unimaginative that money and office filled him with satisfaction.

"Men from the medical society dined with us, too, and members of the bar, and professors from the city university. There were fewer of the last year by year. Rob grew to prefer the company of legislators and bankers, who would laugh like schoolboys at his Irish and Negro stories. We lost more than one nurse who couldn't bear his mimicry.

"I married him in part for his humor, but there is no denying that it grew less genial as he grew older. I married the man who told me those hilarious stories about a common soldier's life, about the lengths he himself had gone to to keep his socks dry, about the gulling of officers, and the dares his comrades took for a draught of whisky.

"I remember laughing helpless throughout one long Sunday afternoon, until Daddy came down to remonstrate with me that brother was at that moment under Yankee guns. After that I removed our interviews from the front porch to the riverbank below the house. It was there, some months later, that Rob asked me to marry him when the war was over. I thought that his proposal would come on a certain Thursday. He was so grave that day. The pauses and hesitancies and vague looks into the middle distance gave away his intentions long before the words came to him. Some inertia though, some lassitude caused him to temporize for nearly a week beyond that day.

"Until then he had dared anything. It was seldom the romantic nonsense that Rose tells company. She creates a man who never existed. But when he cared nothing for the consequences, he was spirited."

A breeze blew through the house, stirring the curtains. It lifted wisps of Lucy's gray hair, like a lover's first tentative gesture.

"Indeed, he became a newspaper editor without peer in the South. But I did not admire him anymore. Nor do I care for the china that his wealth and high seriousness bought for me. I would have been happier with the witty volumes that went unwritten than with the dusty bound reams of newsprint; happier with his suitor's love—I was the center of *that*—than with all his husband's providence.

"Rose requires her myths, of course, especially since she lost the boys' father and then the paper after the Crash. But I could not speak without denying everything she imagines about Rob."

The ancient eyelids, heavy as clockwork, slowly closed, opened, closed again. Lucy's head began to nod.

"Not that anyone has ever paid the slightest attention to me. . .I wonder whether President Roosevelt will send me a telegram on my hundredth birthday. . . ?"

Andrew walked on through the sunlit grass until he was out of sight of the house. Now and then he broke off from its stalk the rounded crown of a thistle and twirled it in his fingers.

Mama would get over the plate, he knew, and when she did she would want to make up to him with some special kindness. She simply could not say that she, too, was sorry, that some things happened for which there was no help and no fault. Her gesture to him would be childlike, filling him with a vague discontent and anger.

There was a whirring of wings and a flash of sunlight on white-and-mottled brown—a bobwhite. The bird stirred him, and he watched her climb. He knew the life close to the surface of the ground. Later, in the summer he could lie for hours on the ground and watch ants make their way through a universe of crossed grass. The earth was still cold to the touch now. Dampness seeped up.

But the bird had been there, keeping her nest warm with her belly.

"Byron would have shot her with that damn gun," he thought.

The path through the field would lead him to, then across the Thorneberry property, along an old railroad bed, then to the highway that passed the church where his grandfather was buried. On his tramp there were many secret treasure places, like the hollow stump where rain collected and toadstools sprouted in the moist, pulpy earth.

His path also passed a giant oak where Andrew had bested his brother on Byron's own terms. The contest had been to see who could sail a rock through the two forks that held up the canopy of the tree. Andrew had chosen a heavy dun stone, smooth on one end, jagged on the other. Gripping the angular surface in his palm, he hurled. Low. End over end it whirred, and chunked firmly into the crotch of the fork. Byron's stone sailed through, but it was a lesser triumph, and soon he found some other testing ground.

The enfolding of the rock by the tree was another of the woods' mysteries that invited him whenever he felt pinned and fixed by the certitudes of the house.

"People are people," Mama would say. Or: "I don't care where you go, people are all the same." Andrew understood that it was because she could not imagine anyone very different from herself. Even the chinaman in pigtails or the pygmy that grinned up at her from the pages of the missionary society bulletin were her brethren, as long as they were at such a far remove from her parlor.

He had to step back and consider a thing for himself. Manners helped make that possible, although Mama never suspected. If you kept up the forms, you could hide behind them.

When there was no form to help—when you broke a dish from Grandmother Lucy's china—you had the woods to run to. Here you could marvel at alien things, things as utterly foreign as it was possible to be. And you could let them keep their differences. There was the slug's glistening trail, and the dead limb that had defied three winters, suddenly lying wet and sweet-smelling in the path after a hard rain.

His brother could make him forget his manners. But if he were careful not to let that happen, he might be every bit Byron's competitor, and then some.

Andrew reached the oak and gazed up at the dull face of the stone, still barely visible. "Mama says that Grandfather Thompson was at home on both sides of the Atlantic," he thought. "His old library is still in the attic. If I got some of those books and learned French, when we go visiting Eleanor in New Orleans, I could order for her in a restaurant."

Very soon it seemed the rock would be enfolded by the fibrous heart of the tree.

The first night after their company arrived, Byron waited until Andrew went downstairs. Sure enough, Mama gave his brother the supper tray to carry into Grandmother Lucy.

Pretending to study the wallpaper, he shuffled through the middle room while Andrew was adjusting the old lady's lapboard. At the door, he sprang forward through the kitchen. At the dining table there were two vacant chairs, one on Eleanor's right, the other opposite her across the red-and-white checkered tablecloth. He surveyed the whole table, up and down, feigned hesitation, then took the chair next to his cousin.

To save ration coupons Mama had mastered a dozen ways to prepare macaroni. Byron often insisted that he could bring home a rabbit or a squirrel, but Mama would not consider it. No member of this family had ever had to subsist on game he killed himself, she said. That was not counting those among the colonists, of course, but within two generations Thompson men were hunting only quarry they took in sport.

Andrew ate what he pleased and kept quiet about it. Tonight there was the distraction of Uncle Jerry's talk, as he showed Andrew how to wield a blowtorch.

Like the trembling of leaves, Eleanor's brown curls danced at the corner of Andrew's eye, as she nodded to show interest when talk turned to Byron's hunting stories. It was a brittle gesture. She was not fully accomplished in it. She had no substantial being yet to give or lend, although she was steeped in the inclination to do those things and arranged her features to allow the viewer to see in them whatever he wanted. Her pallor, the fineness of her hair, her tiny blue eyes that blinked in nervousness made a satisfying prettiness. Her hands were like the inner surfaces of shells.

Andrew spoke up. "I've been practicing my French, Aunt Junie," he said. "When we come visit you all, we can go out to eat in a French restaurant, and I can order for us. I bet you my cousin here would really like some of that pastry. I could tell what the different kinds are."

Eleanor's smile in his direction was guileless, the unawares smile of a young woman sewing as she sat in a window.

"Why, that'd be real nice, Andy, honey," said Aunt Juno. "I don't 'parlez vous' much myself."

"And if we got lost in the French Quarter, I could ask directions—"

"Maybe you'd better leave that French Quarter to me, Andy boy," Uncle Jerry said, raising and lowering his bushy eyebrows. Eleanor giggled.

Mama had been sipping from her coffee, resting her elbows on the table and holding the cup in both hands. Quickly she settled it back to its saucer and sat up straight in her chair.

"Has Juno ever told you, Gerald, that our ancestors were probably Norman? I believe some of us fought with William at Hastings. Our father certainly came by his fluency naturally. Have you seen the scrapbook of his dispatches from Lookout Mountain and Atlanta? Most of his readers failed to grasp his puns in French, but those columns of his lightened some dark days for the best people in this city. After the war, when the state was negotiating to sell pig iron to the Third Republic, he wrote the letter for the Governor's signature. Many an evening they took dinner over this very china—"

Lucy lay listening as the voices rose and fell amid the clatter of utensils. Outside the open window, there were other voices, the bursting open of blossoms, the whimpering of whistlepig pups, the eddying of water in the creek that was swollen by frostmelt. Tonight it would be late before the last wing was furled and tiny hearts slowed in sleep. Singing would go on until after midnight in the woods. Chipmunks would cower in the grassy hillocks, hiding their shining eyes from predators, but barking lowly from field to field.

"Dear Andrew," Lucy thought. "Like your grandfather, you'd sweeten life with a chocolate and a *bon mot*. What kind of suitor will you be, I wonder? Will you last the course? Or will you, as he did, ply your troth, then look away. I know that after he pledged himself that Sunday afternoon by the river, his smile must have faded before he reached the street. From behind the bougainvillea, I watched his steps quicken toward the newspaper office.

"And you, Byron. You resemble the man he became, the protector, the frugal man of business. I lay alone at midnight, while he waited on the latest dispatch over the telegraph wire. Kingdoms crumbled, parties fell—he tried their causes like a chancellor, in the company of that corrupt and dreary miscreant whom the people elected governor. And I lay alone.

"Rose, daughter, I wonder what you would say if you had seen those days? In the same hour when 'the best people of the city,' as you put it, were relishing your father's puns, the freedmen encamped in trenches were eating steamed slabs of opossum, wrapping it in his newspaper to protect their hands from the hot grease.

"That was the first winter after our marriage. All night I could see the Negroes' fires ringing the city, as I lay awake. Gradually the glow from our own hearth faded and died, and the night chill settled about the house. We had made no peace."

Lucy turned her head until her cheek rested against her pillow. Her face looked up into the ever-brightening moon.

"And, of course, he will be remembered long after I am forgotten. I wonder if they even tend my side of the grave we will share?"

With her fingertips she groped about the base of her chair until she found her cane. When she stood her smock hung loosely from her rounded shoulders. She could barely raise her slippers, and silently they traced a path against the nap of the rug.

She closed the screen door quietly behind her, and by turning each time in a half circle, she descended the steps one by one. Beyond the corner of the house, her shuffling form passed beneath the dining room window, the cane sinking into the soft earth and trembling under her. She set out in the direction of the cemetery.

"Grandmother's not in her room!" Byron said from the doorway of the kitchen. He had been sent to fetch Lucy's tray.

"Probably just gone out for her constitutional," said Uncle Jerry. He had helped himself to the last of the coffee, and was peering out the window while he sipped.

Mama went to see about her mother for herself, but indeed Lucy was not in her chair, nor in the parlor.

"Wherever she is, she's taken her cane," Mama said. "Eleanor, dear, would you go see if she's upstairs? Although surely we would have heard her going up the steps."

"We don't get nights like this in Detroit," Uncle Jerry mused. "Everywhere you look, there's a building or a car. Probably she just went for a walk. We all ought to go walking. Good for the digestion."

"Surely she has not left the place this time of night, Gerald," Mama said. "Why, she hasn't even been out of the house since Father's funeral."

In another minute Eleanor bounded into the room. "I looked all over, Aunt Rose. Even in the closets. She's not up there."

"I bet you didn't look in the attic, did you, cuz?" Byron said. "It's awfully dark in there. But don't let Andy fool you with all his stories about secret treasures and spirits and stuff. If you hear the floor creaking at night, it's only a ghost."

"There's no such thing," Eleanor said quickly.

"Well, maybe not where you come from—" Andrew joined in the teasing.

"And not in your old attic either, smarty!"

The girl's hilarity primed her aunt's tears. They welled up at the corner of her eyes. "There is a time and place for fun, children, and this is most definitely not it. Your grandmother is very old and has no business wandering around after dark." Her fingers flitted to her hair, brushed her cheek, gripped and twisted a fold of her dress.

"Oh, Gerald, what must I do?" she begged.

"Take it easy, Rose," Uncle Jerry said. His hand came naturally to her elbow, and he guided her to a chair. "Ellie, fix your aunt some more coffee. Andy, Byron, let's ease down by the road and see if we can see your grandmother. She can't have gotten far."

Byron retrieved the flashlight from a drawer in the cabinet that held bolts and screws, odd lengths of wire, fuses, washers, and little metal parts whose use no one remembered. He and his uncle went on ahead, while Andrew hung back in the doorway. The unshaded bulb suspended from the ceiling by a chain threw his shadow on the linoleum.

Eleanor stood at the stove, passing the pan of water back and forth across the flame. She was as unaware of her movements as a newborn animal. Andrew gazed at her brown curls, like grass stirring in the wind.

"Hey, Ellie," he said. "There aren't any ghosts around here, really. But there are magic things, only you have to know where to look. I'll show you sometime."

The water was beginning to boil. She looked up at her cousin with a bright, uncomprehending smile.

"Okay?" Andrew asked, and grinned. Then he turned and ran through the dark middle room and the parlor. The porch light was on, and insects were thumping against the screen. He threw open the door without slowing, and it banged shut behind him.

"Oh, Andrew!" Mama said, and took the old china cup in her trembling hands.

Lucy had started out in the direction she knew and had wandered into a thicket by the henhouse. A path had once led there and thence up to the highway. But since they no longer kept hens, brambles had reared up, scraping the single filthy pane of glass. In the low night wind the rafters, still encrusted with ancient droppings, twisted and creaked.

When Lucy realized she was lost and turned to go back, a thorny stalk whipped across her cheek. Her feet could find no way not barred by roots or runners. When she tried to step forward, briars as sharp as pens caught her smock, and she pitched to the ground like a sack of grain. The scent of her presence wafted over the field, and the night things stilled, from full cry, to whisper, to silence.

Across the yard came the wavering light and Byron and Andrew calling, "Grandmother! Grandmother!" Lucy heard them and groped for her cane. Her fingernails made a fine tracery in the mud.

The search party looked first in the orchard, where the blossoming trees stood in formation. They directed the beam of light down each row. Andrew stopped for a moment, intrigued by the strange familiarity of the place in this alien light. The flashlight played on the boles and whorls of the trunks that took on the shape of an old woman. Phantasms of Grandmother Lucy sat sprawled between each trunk or shuffled, hunched and lumbering, just out of sight, where the shaft of light melded into the outer dark.

Uncle Jerry was sure she had started toward town. "Well, it sure beats me," he said, when they did not find her on the road or in the ditch.

"Maybe she fell into the pond," Byron said. "Or in the old cistern. It never was filled in good."

It was Andrew who wondered out loud whether she had gone to visit Grandfather Summer's grave on a moonlit night.

"Okay, boys, let's take a look," said Uncle Jerry.

Byron said he would go by the new path, since he had taken his gun that way all winter. He started out, while Andrew and Uncle Jerry, with the flashlight, made their way toward the old henhouse. The moon strewed light between the trees. In the dark intervals, or when something scurried in the undergrowth, Byron called after his grandmother in a voice even louder than before.

He had not gone far when Andrew yelled, "Byron! Come back! We found her!"

By getting on his knees in the mud and grass, Uncle Jerry was able to reach his arm under the old lady and raise her to her feet. She stood, wavering, until Andrew plunked her cane out of the mire and guided its handle into her fist. As they turned her in the direction of the house, the hem of her smock ripped from the nettles.

"Now what made you want to go off like that?" Uncle Jerry asked, draping her arm around his neck and grasping her around the waste. "Hang on, now, we'll get you home, and Rose will get you some dry clothes."

Dangling from the shoulders of her grand son-in-law, Lucy bobbed slowly up and down with their slow forward progress over the uneven ground. Andrew trailed at her elbow.

She had basked in their attention, in the calling voices that had faded and then returned. She might have answered, "Here I am." But then she would have been lost again, permanently and completely lost. If she spoke once, even to save her life, she would have to speak again. And all speech was reproach—to Rose's view of the past—or else it was illusion, for she knew in her silent bitterness that she was only accidentally kin to these insufficient heirs.

Byron joined his brother, and the four of them crossed into the yard just as Mama and Eleanor and Aunt Juno came hurrying onto the porch. Moths and candleflies were making mindless circles around the light and brushing their dusty wings against the ceiling. Mama walked down to the bottom step and peered out toward the light.

"Is she all right, Gerald?" she called out.

"Course she is," he said when they had come a little closer. "Did you ever know Miss Lucy to be anything but all right?"

"Oh, Mama, Mama," Rose said. "Why on earth? What if you

had fallen and broken a bone?"

Uncle Jerry carried Lucy up the steps, while Eleanor dragged a porch chair bouncing noisily across the floor. When they eased her into her seat, it rocked for a moment. Then she sat still, staring straight ahead, her lips drawn in a thin, hard line. Byron stepped to the railing and craned his neck over the hedge to see what it was that held her gaze.

Uncle Jerry, breathing hard, began explaining to Mama that Grandmother Lucy had in fact fallen but that she could not have broken anything because she still had good motor control.

Lucy's left arm slipped over the side of her chair. There it dangled, like a limb broken from a tree. Slowly, her other hand began to rise. It trembled from the wrist at first. The wrinkled forearm followed, swaying back and forth, as if Lucy gripped a pen to expunge a record written on the air.

Finally, the yellow fingers touched Eleanor's shoulder.

A smile flitted tentatively over the girl's face. She looked toward her father, her mother, Aunt Rose, to avoid the blinking amphibian eyes. Lucy's hand opened, taking the contour of her shoulder, tightened.

"Are you okay, Grandma," Ellie asked, bending under the pull of the thin, strong arm.

Lucy brought the girl's ear near. A dry, sibilant whisper rushed over her over her lips, then the corners turned up in a sleepy smile.

Eleanor cocked her head and peered into her grandmother's face. Then she began to giggle. When she raised up to gape at her cousins, the shrill notes rose in her throat and gathered into laughter. It broke over Byron and Andrew, who stared at their cousin until the tears began running down her face.

Her laughter rolled out into the night. The air had grown sweeter by the hour, as pink blossoms lay themselves open and pale green leaves unfurled from the bud. The sugar in their veins gathered, while wings that beat the air strained outward from a plane of glistening eyes, a sac of hollow bones.

The fields were hurrying away from the lighted house, from

the porch where the stick figures stood, when Eleanor's laughter caught in her throat and stopped.

Grandmother Lucy's chin had settled to her chest, which had ceased to rise and fall.

BARGAINS

In August three months before she turned 59, Margie Witherspoon held a yard sale together with her neighbor Mrs. Stanley Nowlan. With help from Margie's son, Hardy, Jr., they carted down from the attic his father's golf clubs and carpentry tools, then carried Stanley's and space lamp and draftsman's rules out from the room that had been his home studio.

They held the sale in the Nowlan yard, because it was on the corner, and passersby could see the signs from both streets. Margie and Peggy Nowlan borrowed cardtables from their women's club and placed them neatly in rows under the maple trees.

In Hardy's things Margie found much she had never known about her husband of 27 years. There was a travel diary of a trip to Rome that he had taken at Christmas 1951—years before they'd met—with a woman whom he had never mentioned but whom he had loved passionately. Then there were spiral-bound notebooks, the kind on display in back-to-school sales racks. Hardy had obviously kept them in his law office, for here in his handwriting were musings about his cases, snippets of conversation overheard in elevators, odd little third-person reflections that were obviously about himself. She mentioned nothing of the writings to Peggy.

Frederick's archives held plans of the City Centre, the building he considered his masterpiece But who would be interested in buying blueprints? They stacked the cardboard tubes in the trash cans at the alley, like rounds in a pistol chamber. Nothing in these effects suggested an interior life, except his class ring which he gave Peggy until he could afford a diamond on installment.

Peggy bundled up her husband's professional papers to send to his surviving partner, but folded and put away the newspaper articles about City Centre's dedication. The building, once a landmark of the downtown, had long been overtopped and was now state offices.

The biggest job getting ready for the sale was the books. Margie and Hardy, Jr. stacked them on the tables, spines up, bracing the ends of the rows with law dictionaries and digests of appellate decisions.

A dollar was the most anybody'd pay for even the best of these old books, Margie thought to herself. She and Peggy sorted the mystery stories and true-crime thrillers that Hardy had fallen asleep to, and made a cardboard sign with a magic marker. "$ Books" and "2-for-a-$ Books." As she taped the signs to tables, a strand of her curly, copper-colored hair wilted in the heat and cascaded alongside her cheek.

Margie was emptying one of the last boxes when one of the books caught her eye. Its jacket was torn at the bottom exposing its scruffed, dun-colored binding. She set aside the stack in her arms and picked up *Great Southern Trials*.

It was not Hardy's but hers, although it had fitted naturally and innocently into their library, shelved with his. Its author was a man from Atlanta, who sent it to her when it was just published, a time when they were writing each other every day. She pressed the dusty jacket against her apron and wiped it clean.

There was a brick arch over a walk leading from the front yard to the deck and pool patio back of the house. She stepped under the graceful curve that Frederick Nolan had designed and into the shadow of the house. The yard beyond stretched in the sun, an emerald sea.

"My beau," she said softly to herself. That's how he had signed his letters. And she opened his book. The once substantial binding creaked now, and the pages had turned brown along the outer edges.

"Mom, we forgot to put a price on this." Hardy, Jr. had seen her go and caught up with her now. She shut the book and stepped back out into the sale area.

Her son was holding his father's humidor. With him was a man her age with a gray beard. He wore an Eagles tee shirt, shorts, and sandals.

Margie held her beau's book stiffly at her side. She felt light and ephemeral, with the thought that all the mastery in all the books of all time were, like love, a match that flared, flickered, and went dark, to burn no more.

She tried to smile at the bearded man. "Oh. . . ," she said, barely above a whisper. "I don't know. Five dollars?"

"How 'bout three fifty?" he said.

"Sure. Fine." The man handed a five dollar bill to Hardy nonetheless, and waited while his change was counted.

Peggy appeared at Margie's elbow out of nowhere. "Looks like we're going to have a good day, 'podner," she said brightly. Her shirt was plastered against her chest by sweat. Soon they would be free of men's things and the memories those things held, gradually becoming old women, tending their gardens of showy flowers inside borders of upturned brick, each secretly competing to grow the largest irises, the frilliest snapdragons, the peonies with the most complex layers.

"Here." Margie held up the book. "I found this." She handed it to Peggy, who took it in freckled fingers.

Roger had said he would write in it for her sometime, but he never did. He had loved her better than anyone ever had, for a long time. She wondered what became of him.

"Let's put it on the dollar table," Peggy said, and without waiting, toddled off.

Thrift store dealers came late in the day and offered prices on the lot of things unsold. They women divided half-and-half the $734 in cash and change. By her beau's prudent, absent hand, he had left his name and hers forever unlinked, never bound by declaration, not in the covers of his book, not anywhere, ever. No one would have bought a book signed to someone else, but a dollar of the proceeds must have been for *Great Southern Trials* for it was gone.

THE GENTLEMEN'S HOUR

The order of business called for a decision about the easement across the redoubt where one hundred and seventeen black soldiers had died in the Civil War, defending the city from capture. But the meeting was late getting started because President Scott Hoyle had spent the night with Christie and she wouldn't let him leave. He sent gravel flying as he pealed out of the driveway of the trailer park, ran a light, and turned his BMW onto the ramp of the inner loop heading downtown.

Christie had even kept Scotty from his appointment at Supercuts, where for fifty dollars every other Thursday Janelle would touch out the gray. He liked the way Janelle let her fingers linger in his hair. He figured she probably wanted him to ask her out, and maybe he would. Another easy mark for this professor.

Thus Riley Harrison reached the historical society's conference room before Hoyle but after everyone else had arrived. All the chairs around the table were taken except the one next to Jimmie Blue, the newest member and the first of his race to sit on the society board. Riley's grandfather had founded a life insurance company which sold debit policies to those people and had made him immensely wealthy. Now the money was Riley's, and he was not going to sit next to Jimmie Blue. Harrison took the president's lateness as an excuse to leave and went across Union Street to the Capitol Club, where Jimmie Blue would never go, and where it was always 1955.

Drury Foster had taken the chair by the cabinet that held the society's official seal, used to emboss invitations to the annual meeting and for various certificates and commendations awarded to potential donors. Drury's face had the texture of a crabapple. He generally wore coke-bottle glasses when working in the society's manuscript collections, out of which he'd written fourteen books, including *The Fascinating Lumber Business* and *Forgotten Hot Springs of Our State.* The society had given him certificates, too, and stored most of the books in the broom closet off the ladies' room.

He had not been aware of Riley's flitting entrance and exit, so they did not exchange greetings. Both had been presidents of every history group in the state, but deciding about this easement was the biggest work either had ever faced in those jobs. Drury was glad the young professor was in the chair. The clock struck four, and Drury realized Scott must have been held up after class, giving special help or explaining a point.

Something in the book she was reading made Grace Haygood, sitting opposite Drury, giggle just then. Giggling was not something a fifty-three year old librarian did with much dignity, Foster thought. In her youth, she had filed the last breach-of-promise suit ever before a Tennessee court. A spinster since the suit's dismissal, she took up community work, volunteering at the animal shelter, adopting dogs that faced being put down because they were ugly or bad-tempered and no one would have them.

Foster was glad that legal anachronism was no more, or son Jim would be in constant need of good defense counsel. That would have been at the bank among the several cashier ladies to whom he'd promised a commitment. Drury was the institution's president and Jim, by sheer dint of hard work and prudent management, had worked his way up to head the mortgage lending operation.

Warren Whitfield, the society's counsel, sat to Drury's left. A few month's back, the society had received for its journal a manuscript linking Whitfield's father to a phony securities deal and a murder that grew out of it. They'd rejected the article for publication, of course, but Whitfield worried that it might turn up somewhere else, on talk radio, the tabloids, anywhere. The lawyer had taken to drink a little earlier in the afternoon. By the time of the evening when his favorite show, Rumpole of Old Bailey, came on, his eye lids were drooping and a dreamy smile across his jowly face. He gave the PBS affiliate $5,000 a year on the condition that they always carry the series and not run anything about queers.

Fortunately, State Senator James Hoagland, who sat next to Whitfield wouldn't notice the flask as the lawyer deftly drew it from his coat pocket and poured a tad into his bicentennial coffee mug, which the society had commissioned and sold. That was because the senator nearly always dozed through the meetings. Sometimes the senator dreamed. Often it was about his wife and when he had first seen her, standing by her daddy's plane, her long raven hair streaming out from the wash of the propellers. It was not only her daddy's plane, but his pasture, which he was subdividing and selling off for a suburb. Then there was Daddy's mountain land in the coal mining district. The senator could have written the society a check to carry out all its business but then he would have had to listen at these meetings. As it was he could doze and just put in a little sweetener when the appropriations bill came up each spring.

Finally, in the middle sat Jimmie Blue. He had not noticed Riley's snub because his attention was concentrated on the single sheet of paper on the table in front of him. He had drawn it from the pocket inside his jacket and now as they waited for Scott Hoyle he smoothed it out on the polished surface of the society's conference table.

Ordinarily on the drive from Christie's trailer park to downtown the president of the society would have commented to himself on the passing scene. He liked to note where the former governor's mansion had once stood, on the Popeye's Fried Chicken parking lot. But in his hurry he scarcely glanced at the waterfront historic district, one of the old warehouses recently converted for a Hard Rock Cafe. The garage where he finally parked had once been Vauxhall gardens, an urban park amid the saloons and dry goods houses of the late nineteenth century city. The board kept on their letterhead a motto meant to remind everyone about these things: "Preserving your heritage since 1849."

Finally, he whisked into the meeting room and took the only seat available. "Sorry I'm late," he mumbled, and then he realized that he'd forgotten his agenda. He leaned over and whispered, "Dr. Blue, may I look on with you?" glancing at the sheet of paper.

In the meantime Kathleen Keisart, the society's executive director, had retrieved another copy of the agenda and placed it at the professor's elbow, with a gesture much like a waiter's in an expensive restaurant, as nearly invisible as possible. Scottie had hired her because she was the most nearly comely of the three applicants for the job. With the ideal of professionalism before her, and the word in her every second sentence, she was prompt about composing the agenda and signing Hoyle's name on it.

As Kathleen receded from the table to her seat, Jimmie Blue picked up the piece of paper before him slowly turned in his chair to face

"There is only one item today, Mr. President. The easement at the redoubt."

Scott leaned forward and placed his palms on the polished table. He looked around the room.

"Discussion?"

Jimmie Blue stood up.

"Mr. President, I rise on a point of personal privilege. If we're going to destroy that ground, I think we should at least have in the official record of this society the names of the men who died there."

"Now, Jimmie, nobody's said anything about destroying. . . ."

"I'd like to read them into the minutes." And he began to do so, pausing briefly after each one.

"Private James Anthony, Third Infantry Company, United States Colored Troops."

"Sergeant Thomas A. Barrow, Third Infantry Company, United States Colored Troops."

"Sergeant Robert Turner Beadle, Third Infantry Company, United States Colored Troops."

Scott would have asked Jimmie Blue just to hand him the list for printing in the minutes, but who else could they get if he got angry and quit, and Hoyle didn't want the society to get into trouble with the affirmative action people. So Professor Blue continued to read, while Drury Foster looked down at his liver-spotted hands, Warren Whitfield leaned back in his chair as a warm glow seeped over his features, and Senator Hoagland's head began to loll toward his chest.

Across the street at the Capitol Club, Riley asked Sam to pour him a second toddy, "only this time with a little less freshet." Riley reminded himself that he must ask Sam his last name sometime and whether he had a family. When he had drunk his bourbon, he started back toward the Society's rooms. All he had to do to pick up the honorarium was to be recorded as present, and that'd cover the bar tab.

Riley stepped out into the late afternoon light on Charlotte Avenue and the light of the late afternoon sun dazzled him. He stared down at his feet for a minute, at the day's paper blowing in the gutter until his eyes grew used to the blazing afternoon sun. Crossing the street and taking a left at the statue of Sergeant York he began to whistle. He remembered his grandfather's story about the legions of men marching this way in the parade they gave the returning troops after the Armistice. His grandfather's company was only a few years old, and he had paid out a near-ruinous amount of premiums on policies that had been written in peacetime. He'd also been forced to take afternoons out for funerals for those with rank of colonel and above.

The state workers had gone home, and the long corridors of the building were shut and silent. Only at the far end a member of the cleaning crew was dragging a trolley of mops and buckets into the corridor. Riley's whistled tune played weirdly off the marble walls with their portraits of dead governors in *faux* gold frames and dangling maroon tassels.

He stopped outside the door, and listened as Jimmie Blue intoned the names. "Lord have mercy!" Riley muttered, "It's not worth it for a couple of watered-down drinks." He sat down on a bench under the portrait of Governor Aaron Tolbert, an old sybarite and seducer, whose fiddle-playing got him elected to three terms in the statehouse, where he'd disfranchised Jimmie Blue's people and gone on to the U. S. Senate.

Grace heard the tune die out. Her beau had stopped his jaunty whistling in the days before his announcing to her that he was throwing her over for that tramp from Clarksville, who had a car. I had no car, she thought to herself, I was proud to walk every day to Peabody or take the streetcar on rainy days.

It was all for the best, she thought, as she had ten thousand times. My animals are what I was given to love. She smiled , thinking of Frisky, her latest mongrel, who'd lost a leg to a car. She'd stop by the convenience store across the street, the one with the historical marker in front marking the site of President James K. Polk's home, and pick up some of those beef strips.

Warren Whitfield had caught the martial air in Riley's tune. and it caused him to focus his attention. He happened to look up into Grace's smile. She must have been pretty once, he realized. He raised his bicentennial mug and winked at her. She looked down but he noted that she continued to smile. And he thought, Why, these are loyal friends, the best friends a man could have.

Drury Foster knew his friend would wait outside now, until Jimmie Blue had finished reading. Blue was a young man, full of ideals. Young men love, or go to war, and since they lived at a moment when there were no enemies to fight, son Jim only did what young men did. His way, as it had been Grace's fiancé's, was the way of the world.

Senator Hoagland, was dreaming of the raven-haired beauty and the mountain land. He had married her, and they had had five children, and he had come a long way in politics, to the chairmanship of the committee on ways and means. He was an old man and his life with his wife was still sweet congress, before the adjournment *sine die*.

His head dipped, his chin brushed his chest, and his glasses fell from his face and clattered onto the table. He drew back, awake now, recovering his dignity with a little-boy apologetic grin. At the disturbance, Jimmie Blue had stopped reading, and Senator Hoagland, groping for the glasses, looked over at Hoyle.

"Move approval," he said.

Scotty was not aware that there'd been a motion on the floor, but he was always attentive to the ways and means chairman, whom he remembered to thank every year for the subsidy and pledge the society's fealty to the state.

"All in favor?" Hoyle asked. There was a chorus of wheezing, muffled, chirpy 'Ayes.' Jimmie Blue shook his head, which Kathleen recorded as 'No' on the motion.

As she always did, she would prepare the minutes, and revise them as Hoyle directed the meeting went. He knew she considered it a real, professional opportunity to work with the professor, just as Christie figured he'd take her out of the trailer park and set her up on the respectable east end of town.

Of course they'd grant the easement for those nice young fellows who wanted to put in the mini-mall. He'd already decided. It was the way things got done, and they'd promised the society a little consideration in it for the endowment fund.

"Move we adjourn," someone mumbled, and each one pushed back his chair and stood, except Jimmie Blue who sat still, his lips drawn thinly, his darkly handsome face impassive.

There was the usual asking after families, and children's marriages and promotions. Then the others filed out into the light receding across the legislative plaza, to fight the good fight, to keep the faith of their fathers.

TAKING POSSESSION

"A big plastic nose?" Allen said. "Come on! I'm just teasing you."

They were sitting on the pallet. Leigh had the covers pulled up around her. Since the mugging Allen had been sipping on a tumbler of wine. Although he felt fine, he had not minded the excuse to drink early in the evening.

Leigh was listening to his plan, if he had been the robber. After he'd grabbed the wallet, he'd have run into an alley and hid in a garden. He'd have worn something beside a pastel blue running suit. But first, he'd have gone to a costume shop and gotten a clever disguise. Big glasses—he held his palms on both sides of his face—and one of those big noses.

"Mmmmmm," Leigh said. "It might have worked."

When he told her he was joking, she lunged at him and hit him in the chest with the side of her fist. "Oh, you!"

"You're always making things up," she said. "Have you ever lied to me?"

It was one of those wifely questions that Allen had learned to be wary of in the first months of their life together.

He thought about the time he was sitting in Leigh's pink wingback chair, trying to write a poem to her faculty colleague, not because he loved Leigh less nor Anna more. It was only Anna's fetching face, about which Southern poets and old balladeers once wrote, before lyricism had gone out of the world.

He sat, shoeless, trying for words that were like the carved tusks in the exhibit of Eskimo art that he and Leigh had seen at a Georgetown gallery.

"I'm writing an unignorable poem," he said to his fiancee when she asked what he was doing. That had been one hopeless truth. Another, which he did not tell, was that Anna's face opened new spaces in his mind.

Now Leigh was his wife of six months. For the last half day they had lived in a new home on Capitol Hill, in front of which Allen had just been mugged.

"No, sweetie," he said. "I've never once lied to you."

The down payment had been Leigh's money. She packed all the china, too, and then unloaded it in the hot sun. And she made an early dinner, cold sandwiches and boiled eggs. After all that, he insisted on going out for wine, to drink with the first meal in their new house.

The kitchen at the back looked out on a tiny brick terrace, its profusion of roses confined by a pointed pole fence. From her stove, over the bubbling of water in the pan, Leigh could not hear Allen's growl that rose to a scream and the slap of shoes on cement as he started after the robber.

Allen did not remember setting the wine on the retaining wall out front. When he plodded back to the house, winded, moisture was condensing on the cold surface of the neck. He picked it up and carried it into the kitchen.

He knew that Leigh always worried that he was out meeting someone, so he said, "I've been mugged."

"Oh, Allen!" she ran to him. "Oh, sweetheart, are you all right? Here." She slid a dishtowel under the dripping bottle and sat it on the dining table.

He explained everything from the time when the kid snatched his wallet from the back pocket of his jeans to the point where the patrol car took over the chase. Under his shirt, filthy from sweat, he could feel his heart pounding.

The officer who brought the boy around to be identified told Allen he had been lucky; they'd found no gun. "And that outfit," he said, "You could have spotted it a mile off." He called Leigh "ma'am." She stood in the doorway while two policemen lifted the handcuffed thief out of the back seat. Allen glanced at him and looked away. Both of their faces were impassive.

The towel and the wine were gone by the time Allen and the policeman came inside. Leigh had moved some of the boxes stacked on the cabinet to the floor. The officer declined coffee. To Allen's Leigh added some liqueur, but when he felt his hand trembling, he put the cup down and let it sit.

When the officer completed his report and left, they ate, slowly. Leigh drew him a bath, although he protested that she must be as tired as he was. So he fixed hers afterwards, and going downstairs to the box marked BATH retrieved some bubbly soap and added it.

He was exhausted, his legs heavy as sand, but his mind was leaping of its own accord from image to image of the chase—the figure in the blue running suit ahead of him, the snarls rising from his own gorge.

By the time Leigh came to bed, she had thought the subject through and had come to some conclusions. She changed the subject from lying.

"You were very brave, sweetheart. But, don't you think, a little foolish? That that was one big, fat chance to take?"

Once, not long after they first met, she had described his sending a copy of his journal to her in nearly the same words. She did not remember doing so. Their memories often selected different fragments of the past. She thought the journal betrayed him, his basic confusion in life. In the car on the way to the airport after his first visit, she advised him that there were some things he ought to talk over with professional help.

He called her when he had made the appointment. She said that it was very mature.

Dr. Frobisch turned out to be a Freudian who kept a bodhisattva on his credenza and by his telephone a coin, fastened between two little uprights that read "buy" on one side and "sell" on the other. From Allen's point of view, the psychiatrist worried about the wrong questions. "Why are those feelings coming out now?" Frobisch asked. "Why are you afraid to say that to Leigh?"

They met every week for more than a year, then Allen canceled an appointment and left word that he would not be coming back. It was as though he had been talking about someone not himself, someone beset with trivialities and not he, who had written a journal that was like the carving on scrimshaw.

Allen's lapses of memory were always about important things, such as what he had said to Leigh on the altar at the pause in their wedding service put there for the groom. "It was so beautiful," Leigh said that night. "Write it down for me, please."

Allen wanted to go walking on the beach first, and Leigh reluctantly agreed. They had already established, at her behest weeks before, that they would probably be too tired by the ceremony, the reception, and the drive to make love.

The night was moonless, dry, cold. The waves rushed, broke, and splashed at their feet. Allen wanted to talk about his ancestors, who had made wedding jewelry with shells and, at dawn, pushed their boats into the sea and put to screeching flight the gulls diving over the lavender water. When he saw that his bride was cold, he turned her gently in the direction of their room.

In a drawer was stationery of the First Flight Motel. The embossed crest of its letterhead showed the Wrights and their plane. The choice of this place to stay on their wedding night might have been Allen's whimsy, but it was not. Most places on Cape Hatteras had been closed for the last week of the year.

Using the telephone directory to write on, Allen copied for Leigh what he had declared for her, before all the company assembled, during the high church service. Actually, he had only an approximate idea. He wrote:

> The odds were against this, you know. We came so far
> to find each other, in the face of them. I don't believe any-
> thing could happen that would drive us apart, after such
> confusion and pointlessness. It would be easy, in this mo-

ment, to promise to love you forever. But what I promise is to try to be loving when you feel tired and when you're lonely, when you're no longer as ravishing as you are today, and when we can barely remember when we fell in love, or why, or how.

Leigh put the sheet of stationery with the sachet that her grandmother enclosed with a wedding present. Once she quoted part of it to Allen, who turned a logical objection and provoked his wife to tearful complaint. "But you said it! You did!" Leigh fumed.

He considered telling her the truth, that instead of making love with her on their wedding night, he composed vows that he had not spoken; that, even on the altar, he had imagined mesmerizing one of the fetching bridesmaids with a poem; the he had been exhilarated from the walk on the beach when he wrote the words on the veneered little desk at the First Flight Motel. He said nothing, however, and, in any case, the words were no lie.

They lived at first in Leigh's pretty apartment off Connecticut Avenue. The landlady, with quarters below, sat in the garden every afternoon when spring came, drinking martinis from a silver pitcher. She agreed to watch after Allen's tabby cats, Molly and Mischief, who hid in the grass and bounded after imaginary prey.

He had moved his things in two weeks before the wedding. Leigh asked him to measure his sofa, his bookshelves, and a pigeonhole desk that had once held his grandfather's accounts. She arranged everything perpendicular to the walls and all else in relation to those right angles, managing to keep an arms length between the twin beds. He helped her achieve her plan, a close fit between their two lifetimes' accumulation.

Their own home on Capitol Hill they chose after weeks of pointing out to each other types they liked. Allen preferred building materials of dark color and windows that made a wall. Leigh was for pastels and qualifications. Much depended for her on parts she could not see, the furnace, the flues, tiles under the stove.

The agent admitted that they would be alone as a couple on

the street, among single men and women or long-time residents. But others would be following, he assured them, moving his hands rapidly and jangling his bracelets. Then he steered them to the patio to show them the abundant roses.

The flowers spilled over the pointed, unpainted fence poles, making the tiny patio smaller still. They were the only desirable thing in the neighborhood not subject to theft. Even that was not absolutely true. Another day, when Allen and Leigh were standing in the kitchen with the structural engineer, Leigh watched their neighbor cross the alley, vase in hand, and snip away freely.

Their new home, which was at least a century old, had once been a boardinghouse, the engineer told them. There were old pipes and faucets closed off in the walls, beneath layers of paper, paint, and plaster. Congressmen must have stayed there, Allen imagined; maybe even Lincoln of Illinois. It was theirs now, as was the anxiety of ownership. They placed hopes in the lack of fissures in the foundation, and they delighted in the moldings, the chandelier, the useless pretty designs on the banister.

The night before they actually came to live in the house, they worked late, carrying boxes from the U-Haul up the front steps until past 2 a.m. The wind was blowing through the open windows and doors, and every light on the first floor was ablaze. From Pennsylvania Avenue two blocks away came hilarious, drunken shouting and the whine of engines shifting through their pitches.

With the last crate in his arms Allen stopped at the door, resting the load on a railing that would need rustproofing. At the end of the hall in the fluorescent kitchen, Leigh was unpacking a box with the cereal and coffee.

My wife, Allen said to himself. It seemed very unlikely still.

Standing on the steps of his home, in the night wind in the sleepless city, he realized that his marriage would not be even what was shared but, rather, the memory of sharing. Memory would make the bond that could not be dissolved in distraction or anger. They had to create between themselves a fund of experiences that could be remembered.

For Leigh, the marriage was a gamble, chance taken against her own experience. She was bound, one way or another, to prove something to herself, yes or no, can or can't, to be forever with Allen or forever alone. He was right when he said that everything was one way or another for her. Irony gave her no pleasure, while he basked in it.

Allen trusted his judgment in the flux of the moment, since he was sure that no plan was ever made that did not require some revision. He was perpetually starting over, while Leigh was at every occasion and evaluation, punctilious, organized, and accomplished.

She offered Allen security and the imperial capital, to explore together. She would continue mastering its set ways, while he regarded it, like every space, as open to development. The drawers in his desk overflowed with first paragraphs of stories, lists of books to read, memorable columns of Safire's, and class notes from his alma mater's magazine, names from his year to whom he was always intending to write congratulatory notes on books, babies, on second, presumably happy marriages. The profusion represented his mind, which held numerous unconsummated friendships and more corrupt thoughts than roses on his patio.

In the journal he'd shared with Leigh, he'd tried to infuse every word with a density of meaning, to condense more and more into ever smaller verbal space, to be infinitely allusive. Leigh read his puns and plays on words according to her own anxieties. Her general view was that he had a lot to get over before he could be with her. But in the hours with the psychiatrist he renounced nothing. His experience had been a pathless, and unbordered field. His tropes in the journal were like a kite that he let play out above him.

A "Goody Two-Shoes," Leigh described herself. They had, nonetheless, gone to bed on the night they met, which gratified Allen's love of romantic encounter. They had not made love, which preserved Leigh's sense of and her actual virginity.

It was possible that the marriage was the first thing she had ever begun without knowing the outcome. Ordinarily she knew what would occur and in what order events would happen. Improvisation was intolerable. Once when Allen offered to buy her flowers from a street vendor, he was compelled by her hesitation over some wilted leaves to select the best available bouquet. Another time, they missed a matinee because of the traffic and Leigh began to cry and swear. Allen proposed a walk downtown that eventually ended at a sidewalk cafe. Gradually she took over the plan, even ordering the ice cream, and the activity ceased her unease. But if the marriage plans had gone awry, she would have blamed Allen entirely.

The question of the ring indeed led to their first argument.

"You don't want to wear it because you don't want anyone to know you're married," Leigh accused him. It was a statement out of her distrust and out of the advantage she had gained in knowing his history from his journal.

"Now there's an example of how we're different," Allen said. He wanted to keep the ring on a chain and wear it around his chest. "When I'm reaching for the telephone, or running, and it presses against me, I'll know. I'll feel it next to me, and I'll be reminded of you. For you, it's what other people see and think."

Leigh was drawn gradually toward trust in Allen because of such irritability and such reasoning. If he could be made honestly outraged, he would tell the truth about himself and about her. He knew how to put her in place when he pummeled her with logic. Allen assumed that all women were infinitely resilient, that they never gave up, that they were vulnerable but always forgiving. He was sure that Leigh would never leave him, no matter how hard he might try to abandon her.

Leigh had earned a doctorate in public health from Johns Hopkins with hard, routine labor. She mastered survey techniques, matching respondents' age, sex, and other aspects of themselves they had not chosen with data that they had not understood. It was the farthest thing from interpretation, which was the essence of Allen's work as an historian. She could have been a nun as easily as professor of nursing. He could have been a shortstop, a limnologist, or one of the fellaheen.

Leigh planned every aspect of the wedding not given in the Book of Common Prayer. She did not intend for the date to be necessarily advanced, so for their prim, cool lovemaking during the last months she insisted that they both arrange for contraceptives. She wanted no cuddling, and afterwards went to her own bed.

The priest, Father Emerson, smelled of expensive cologne and embarrassed even Allen with his superficial, faintly leering counseling and the vast, vulgar array of his apartment where he met with the two of them. But he was another, necessary authority for Leigh.

For Allen they would never become all that this pretension implied. But for practical purposes they would seem to, and so Leigh would be pleased, so long as he protected her view and left his relentless double view at the doorstep of their home and their life together.

"I'm formal to avoid confronting my past. You're formal to be in good taste. Is that how it works?" He hurled such questions at her when she doubted his consistency and honesty of purpose. The dance of his mind had nothing, or very little to do with deceit or evasion but with the vital moment. His journal captured this; there was energy there. He had traditions and teachers of whom he wanted to be worthy by going beyond them.

Leigh did not actually need Allen and never would, and she refused this appeal to him, the most persuasive she might have made. Yet his bride delighted him! Every act of love was an unexplored continent. He wanted enough history made together that would hinder his waywardness.

A lot of banter at their parties, like much of their pillow talk, was about courtship. "I thought you were going to walk out at that point," said Leigh. Allen said, "It seemed to me that I was reaching the upper limits of my investment with you." And Leigh revealed, "I decided to sleep with you that first night after you brought me champagne, then left me alone." Mainly clothed but entwined, he later told her that he expected to live a marginal life forever. When he was old his address would be an apartment whose walls were lined with books, "a few of them by me. And alone, except for Molly and Mischief, or their descendants, anyway."

They hurtled toward love, startling them both. "I wanted to tell you that night," Allen said, "but I was afraid I'd frighten you away."

"You would have," Leigh answered.

But he had not been especially wary of sending her the journal, by which he meant to say, I am not frivolous. I want this to go somewhere.

"It's profound," Leigh commented on the manuscript. Then she recommended, for the sake of the relationship, that he see the psychiatrist.

They were slow to achieve any togetherness and agree on a shared, private language. Allen worried that she loved him because he was pliable. Leigh accused him, after they finally became intimate, of "having a good thing going."

Allen gradually took the bearing that seemed required in the city. For a time he remained aware of the poses he struck. His wife, on the other hand, could appear open when she was in full control of the situation. It was the Hopkins training. People forgot that they expected the poses of him, of themselves, of everyone else, so the city was generally blamed. No one denied, however, that it was a beautiful city and one worthy of a great nation, even one whose day was passing.

Leigh was teaching on the evening that the law student from the public defender's office came to take Allen's statement about the mugging. Instead of being glad for the time alone, when he could without risk imagine himself lonely again, he was morose and restless. He asked the student about his courses, and what kind of law he expected to practice. He had learned a great deal from Leigh's charming ways of showing interest in others, and he sensed that some tentative, surging friendship passed between them.

The student wrote, reducing Allen's convoluted, scrupulous sentences into spare nouns, verbs, objects. Allen suggested they go for a beer, since he felt no malice toward the robber and he thought that he and the student should be at a pub singing karaoke. The boy said he had three more cases to interview in the neighborhood.

Before they went to trial, Allen learned that the mugger was a juvenile and that he had two previous convictions, including armed robbery.

The prosecutor was Allen's age, but older, with veiled eyes. It was a point against his official pride when the kid walked with a suspended sentence. Running to the next courtroom, he called to Allen, "Don't worry about it. He'll be back in the system, and when he is, I'll nail him."

It truly did not matter to the victim. In three hours waiting on the witness bench he reread much of Huizinga's *The Autumn of the Middle Ages*, then collected $30 in witness fees. On the Metro returning home, he shivered, perhaps from the air conditioning or the damp that seeped in along the seals of the subtly floodlit walls.

On this evening after the hearing, Leigh was still worried about Allen's having turned on the mugger with such rage. It was what she might have expected from his journal, she thought. It was even more likely than his being unfaithful to her, and a virtual certainty compared to the likelihood that he would pursue a fortune.

Also, she pointed out, he might have been shot to death.

It was his idea, their putting aside some time, early or late, every evening of their lives, for the marriage. He was proud of it, his inventiveness in proposing it, during the engagement, after his initiative for their love was over and Leigh, in her necessity to manage things, had taken control.

They would talk about worries and fears. It was Leigh who brought up the mugger, now working the streets again. She said, "I guess I'm wondering whether you ought to have stopped seeing Dr. Frobisch, with so much anger left in you. Yes, that's it. That's what I'm really worried about."

"For God's sake, Leigh," Allen exploded. "The kid tried to steal my wallet. It just made me mad as hell." For the hundredth time, it seemed to him, he explained to her that he learned with the psychiatrist what he had already known, and she did not give him credit for building an accomplished life on shambles.

"You keep reminding me about the close calls," he said. "My point is that I succeeded. That's another way we're different, for your list. And it worries me, knowing how you really despise people who are different from you."

Leigh, lying on her back with her knees raise, turned toward him. "You've had a lot of pain, sweetheart. And the only way out of it is through it."

His voice rose out of himself, as it had at the robber. "That's another way of saying that I'd be happier if I were more like you." He lifted himself up on his elbow. He tried to order his thoughts, but the words flew out ahead of them, and it was the beginning of the profoundest change until then in their common life.

"You can choose," he said. "There's me as I am, or nothing. If you raise the subject of my mental health again, I won't even leave a forwarding address."

They were still encamped on the floor, Leigh having decided to order the downstairs, public part of their home first. When she turned over and began crying, Allen got up to set the air conditioner on low.

There were no curtains over the windows yet, and the streetlight glowed bright and metallic in the room until the first blur of morning. A contrail from a jet was drawn across the sky in the west, over the monuments. Molly hunched on the sill, fascinated by all she surveyed of the Congressional staffers scurrying to work.

Allen wanted to make love, but Leigh didn't. Then, wary that she had hurt him again, she did and he didn't. "No," he whispered, holding her. "We'll set the stage first. I know you like that."

He fell asleep, and when he woke, his efficient and elegant wife was already downstairs. He could smell bacon frying and hear the crinkle of paper as she unwrapped melons.

He shaved, dressed, and started down. At the window on the stairs he saw their neighbor coming down her garden walk in the direction of the roses, vase in hand.

Allen watched as she pushed open the gate with her knee. He noted the tights, the smooth movement of her legs. He wondered if she were a dancer.

He rapped gently on the glass. The girl looked up to the house's new owner, standing in the window. She smiled brightly and waved. Allen watched as she walked along the alley, pouring the water over the vinca that grew down to the cinders' edge.

CULTURE WARS

Just before I reached the curve in the road, I heard the combo through the trees. A limousine whipped around the blind turn and on past me down the hill, scattering dried leaves over the asphalt. As the car disappeared, a pale braceleted arm fluttered briefly at the window.

Finally I saw the drive, beside which stood a mailbox decorated in art nouveau scrollwork and bearing the name "Dr. Alex Carr." At the hilltop, over the peak of the roof line, yellow stone chimneys answered the late afternoon sun. On the terrace, ringed with lanterns, the band prevailed. A tall bearded fellow—John somebody, from Texas—who sat across from me in Victorian Literature gyrated near the banister. Carr's party had been underway for hours.

The invitation had said, "From 3." But the afternoon shift at the library did not end until 5. I hadn't bothered to go by my room and change clothes.

The envelope, addressed in Carr's handwriting, had been placed in my department box the day after the item appeared in the graduate newsletter about *Dionysius* accepting a story of mine. I almost missed the date. I was seldom in the English building at all, except for the hours a week that I went to class.

I did not join the philological society or sign petitions insisting on departmental reforms. I chose lecture courses over seminars when I could, and I ate in the Union cafeteria rather than at the graduate pub. I studied (and drank a Southern bourbon, a tie with home) in my $50-a-week room and left daisies at the doors of coeds who sometimes became my muse but seldom more. I was not known, not to my professors, not to other students, not even to the receptionist in the English department who guarded the time of Dr. Holberg, our chairman and Twain man. People had difficulty remembering my first name, Timothy, so I was often "Mr. Young."

When I'd applied to the doctoral program at the university, my father asked me, "Why do you want to traipse off way up there, son? If you'd stay here and just go to State, my mother and me, we'd make arrangements for you. We'd like to have you close by now." Sometimes he spoke in the rhythms they keep in the Southern mountains. His speech had made Shakespeare easier for me.

I understood his instinct, in the face of the loss we had recently shared, to take into his thick, sunburned hands what he still had left and pull it inward toward himself. But ever since I was young, languishing in the pastel corridors of our small-town high school, I had longed to attend this university. Its celestial reputation gathered me up, and I, in turn, made it the repository of my ideals.

It was the place, after all, where ideas contended and the best prevailed, where discourse was elevated, and words husbanded. From the bell tower, pictured on the cover of the catalog, I imagined I heard the "Academic Festival Overture." From one cedarn hill to another the music rolled, as across the brick sidewalks men and women in fluttering gowns marched beneath the high-piled clouds of early summer.

As this procession in my mind passed through the cloisters—timeless spaces where the past was always available, hence pliable, changeable, capable of being reshaped—I saw the faces of the women students, soon to receive their degrees in fine arts and be wed to tall young men with settled futures.

And what of the scholars at the head of the parade? They would return, I was sure, to the exegesis of old manuscripts or the ceaseless, selfless testing of hypotheses.

In such a place I would feel at home in the world for the first time. I would live in and through its intellectual rigor, its lancing, cerebral light. At the same time its passionate advocate, I would defend it against those who drew on its reputation without replenishment. Since one living at the boundary sees more acutely than one living within, I declined a proferred stipend and took a work-study job in the university library instead.

In the afternoons I loaded books at the bottom of the chute into a dumbwaiter. Commercial novels by Alec Carr's former students turned up regularly in the pile, some of them bearing a hearty blurb from him on the back cover.

It must have bothered Carr that I had acquired a limited notice, through the acceptance of my story, without his even knowing who I was.

When I entered his living room, he was standing on the far side, one foot upraised and resting on a stone planter. A giant tropical plan caught the sun's last rays. Down below the window wall, the globular lights along North Platte street traced a supple curve over the river and out toward the plains. I negotiated my way around a huddle of sober-faced early admissions freshmen, commenting sardonically on one another's social blunders.

Carr had doffed his jacket and his honor society keys dangled beneath his bulging midriff. His white curly sideburns set off his beaming red face, like one of his saucy parenthetical phrases. The ice in his scotch clinked as he gestured to the circle around him. I recognized one of the teaching assistants, Dionne something from the Bronx. She was tall, with a sallow face, pencil-thin eyebrows, and hair the color of prunes. She was younger than me, as earnest but more strident, with a New Yorker's fortitude.

"Oh, uh, Mr. Young," she said. "I forget your first name—please, join us!"

I was acknowledged by our host with a little nod. We were obviously in the middle of one of the famous Alec Carr's "holding forths," a melange of literary gossip, obscure scholarship, carefully tempered praise, and a final summing up of the book or author under discussion. Many hearers would repeated Alec Carr's last word as their own.

Carr's subject of the hour was a memoir by an East Coast publisher with whom he'd once been associated.

"I add, with considerable qualification, 'intimately,'" Carr noted. The laughter floated above the hubbub of the room.

"Wife and I attended the soiree that Robert gave on the eve of his emigration. It was his last day but one in New York. His last one forever, he was saying then. And it might have been, had he not met the love of his life on the flight over—a willowy, fluttery sort from old Dixie. Her father owned half the town of Thompson, Georgia—I presume that means something to Thompsonians and all you Thompsonphiles. Anyway, the trip was *pater*'s graduation gift, her grand tour in the manner of those antebellum belles, and she had a flight bag packed with brochures of places to do.

"Robert had certainly been somber that night before his departure. Mrs. Carr assured him—and I agreed of course—that there would always be a place for him in the arts in America."

"'Ah, dear Hermione,'" he said, lowering his eyes, 'Love has always dealt so badly by me here. I'm determined to simply write my book. If *she* ever comes, she will, although I no longer believe or expect.'

"Destiny intervened, though, in the form of seating arrangements on the plane. Robert persuaded the girl to throw her brochures into a wastebin at Orly, and together they exhausted the continent. Six weeks later, they were back in the states, both fairly shimmering. And then he did write the book, not the one that would transmute his true love into gold—but rather this lesser, duller thing. If you look at it in the right light, it gives off a satisfactory luster. But real gold, you ask. Oh, no. Oh, my, my no."

Some members of the circle gave out little nods of appreciation. Carr looked about for the waiter. The pupils of his eyes were small and gleaming, like rifle shot. In a moment he had been provided with another drink, and they settled on me.

"You must be Mr. Young. Tell us about your story."

Ordinarily I didn't care to talk about anything I'd written. Carr's question took me by surprise and I stumbled.

"Well, it's about the death of one soldier, in the war, in the spring of 1968. . . ."

"Oh!" said Dionne, the prune-haired girl. "Don't you think people want to forget about all that?"

"Now wait," someone else said. It was John, the fellow who'd been dancing at the porch's edge. He was evidently past his orals and assuming the air of the young professor. I knew him, from seminar, to be a fervent admirer of Henry James. He always felt it was his duty to state all possible sides. We waited, fearfully.

"The subject would appear to be exhausted," he continued, glancing in my direction. "On the other hand, what point of view does his story take? Just because he belonged to an idealistic generation doesn't mean that it's another tiresome protest piece—"

"Oh, you and your everlasting 'point of view'" Dionne interrupted sharp and loud. Were they lovers? I wondered.

Alec Carr quaffed his drink and sat the glass on the rim of the planter. He looked me up and down.

"You certainly don't look like a slogan-shouter to me, Mr. Young, You've obviously come from an honest day's labor. But we're being rude. Do go on with your story."

During the colloquy, I'd lowered my eyes to the floor, feeling for the first time since leaving my father's house a nameless emotion between embarrassment and contempt. At Carr's injunction, however, the circle quieted, and I looked up at John, the Jamesian.

"The story is told through the eyes of a young man," I said, "the brother of the dead soldier. It's his story, as much as his older sibling's.

"He's serious, dissatisfied, restless. He attends the high school in the small town where his parents live. He longs for a wider life, reads newspaper editorials, watch t.v. news every night, wishing he could join the marches in Mississippi. His parents are two disappointed people who talk about what it takes to get by. His father is a land surveyor, his mother keeps house with the help of a maid, once a week. They hope with his interests in books and argument that he'll grow up to be a lawyer.

"He hears the knock on the door first, because the boys' bedroom is at the front of the house. He scrambles down out of the top bunk, which he'd taken over when his brother enlisted, and lifts up a slat of the blind. As soon as he sees the olive-green car, he knows what has happened.

"Rage rushes through him; he's angrier than he has ever been. He tears open the door of his room and sprints around the corner. He's clenching his fist, he's going to hit the officer in the face, as hard as he can, that officer standing in the doorway saying now to his mother, 'I'm sorry, ma'am, your son has been killed in action.'

"Only the soldier is a black man. And he just stops there, not looking at him as he finishes his set piece about the Army's arrangements to bring the body home. He just looks out through the glass door, across the yard, clenching and unclenching his fists. . . ."

Alec Carr stirred, rattling the ice in his glass, which was empty again.

"You must find some way to renew the old verities," Carr declared, plunking his glass down. This time he had to exert himself to locate the edge of the planter.

I did not feel obliged to defend the story; it had been hard enough to write. There was already too much energy expended in empty arguments about literature. The PMLA was tedium become an institution. Silence itself put an infinite distance between me and such futility. I knew also that honest discussion would be useless before the self-absorption of a drunk.

In the summers when I was growing up, I had worked on my father's crew as a rod-and-chain bearer. Afterwards to a man, they stopped off at Millie's Place, while I went into her back room to watch the network news. Sometimes it would be after dark when we got home. There would be two pork chops in the blue gray grease on the stove.

"Wipe your feet, anyway," my mother called out. "The girl will be wanting a raise if she has to do any more than vacuum."

I helped my father with his boots and eased him into his chair at the table. He chattered for awhile, his tongue thick, before he fell asleep. My mother would coax him to bed.

The front room I shared with brother was my refuge from the ennui and despair of this country life, while I dreamed of the university. He sought another exit, in error's army. "Yessir, Timbo, I'm going to go over there and end that war up!"

I heard later that the party broke up about one a.m. with Alec Carr declaiming "Allegro" from the terrace at the top of his lungs. I left long before that, being scheduled for the early shift at the library the next day.

I was shelving books under the skylight on the upper left when a boy with curly red whiskers and eyes that didn't quite focus asked me where to find Alec Carr's books.

"Fiction or non-fiction?" I asked.

He squinted at the crumpled paper in his hand.

"It just says, *The End of the Word.*

"Right. Non-fiction. It's shelved by call number, over there, third row from the end."

"Thanks, man," he said, and gave me a mock salute. As he walked away, his heels struck an irregular tap across the room, another soldier, another parade.

THE PORTRAIT OF A LADY

Birdie Tucker, chairman of the Ladies Heritage Association, swept back the lace curtains and peered out the window of the President's house. A yellow-and-black school bus was moving up the drive toward the portico, spitting gravel into the grass. She squinted through her thick lenses and made out the handprinted sign in the window:

ARCADIA COUNTY FUTURE FARMERS OF
AMERICA.

With a squeal of brakes the bus came to a stop below her. The door spread open on its rubber wheels, and the Future Farmers began to file out. To Birdie Tucker they looked all arms and legs and bug eyes as they mingled about, gaping at the facade of the house that they had seen only on postcards or in history books. One of them, standing in the middle of the driveway with his hands on his hips, settled his foolish stare on her, sitting in the window. She let the curtain fall.

Finally one of the guides came out to start the tour. Birdie Tucker listened carefully as Laura introduced herself. From the rear of the group someone called out, "Got a phone?" Birdie would have liked to slap his sassy face. But she knew Laura was a lady and would keep her poise. Sure enough, the girl went right on to point out the features of the grounds around the house.

The Ladies Heritage Association had made some new revisions in the presentation only a week before at the guides' meeting, held promptly at 8:30 each Monday in the staff room, formerly the President's dinner service pantry. It was that morning that Jennifer Huggins and Kelly Weaver had appeared in those skirts! Birdie Tucker remembered very well. She had made them kneel right before the others and had leaned a ruler against almost two inches of besilked thighs. They'd been told the Ladies' rules about guide skirt length time and again, she declared, and she sent them both home to change. The rest of the girls could she was not to be trifled with that day. Although they slumped and looked thoroughly put out with her, they took the new tour script without a word. They were to have it memorized, she told them, by Tuesday week—today.

One of the best, Laurie had done just as she was told. "That square of stones you see just past the large cedar tree is the original foundation of the smokehouse that served the house in the early 1800s. In those days the family kept a large herd of cattle and processed all the meat for its own use, as well as a surplus that it sold in town. Those operations were curtailed when the President left for Washington, and when the smokehouse caught fire and burned in 1833 it was never rebuilt. . . ."

Birdie Tucker's attention was diverted by one of the Future Farmers who was kicking at the border around the tulip bed. She raised a wrinkled fist to rap on the glass, then thought better of it. What was the use? Every one of them would take something if he could get his hands on it. Better a loose brick than a tassel from one of the portraits in the library. The President's glass doorknobs had been one of the most coveted items, until the Ladies decided to replace them with imitation brass ones. Daisy Belle Hopkins, quietest one of the group though she was, had piped up with the idea one day. And luckily, Flora Adams' husband, Barney, was in the wholesale hardware business and could get them for the Association at cost. "I just try to have a spirit of helpfulness," Daisy Belle said when they applauded the idea. So the Ladies kept a crate of doorknobs on hand, and from time to time Mr. Black, the groundskeeper, fitted one to the rudely exposed gears of a lock.

Sometimes, Birdie Tucker thought, she didn't know which was worse, the tourists who took whatever was lying about or those who insisted on giving the Ladies any amount of bric-a-brac, claiming the President had once touched it, worn it, tread on it, slept under it, or kicked it over in one of his notorious tantrums. The latest gift had arrived that very morning, and Birdie Tucker was sure that the Ladies could have carried on the President's memory very well without it. In fact, it was sure to be trouble, and nothing but trouble.

It was a portrait of the President's wife. Birdie Tucker had been expecting it every day since a lawyer's registered letter arrived, explaining that his late, wealthy client wanted the mansion to have it. When it came—the courier cutting across the grass, provoking Birdie Tucker no end—she had torn away its cardboard cocoon, drawn down the cotton stuffing, taken one luck and caught her breath. Fiercely, hastily she'd packed the wrapping around it and hailed Mr. Black, running his weed eater at the foundation of the President's tomb, to help her get it downstairs.

M. Larry Brown, Ph.D. student and part-time curator, was eating lunch out of a brown paper bag. When the pair entered he looked up from the book he was reading, the latest biography of the President which linked the monetary policies of his administration to the fact of his having had a domineering father.

"What now, Mrs. T.? Looks like a picture. Can I have a look?"

He did, and gave a low whistle. "Just wait till the next time the D.A.R. comes through and gets a load of that."

"I don't want anybody to see it," pronounced Birdie Tucker. "Not for the time being anyway. The girls, uh, the Ladies Association will decide whether it's to hang in the house or not. You just tell us whether it's genuine."

"Sure, Mrs. T. I've already got one of everything else under the sun to research—a prayer book, a peace pipe, a bay rum-and-lavender bottle. Why not a portrait of the First Lady, too? I did get around to that bucket of nails the Historical Society collected from the Ponder County courthouse, the one they're tearing down? We know the President practiced law over there when he was first starting out. It wouldn't have been in that courthouse, though.

Nails like those weren't made till after the Civil War. Most people don't realize that of course. You want Mr. Black to throw them out?"

At first Birdie Tucker said no, that maybe he could use them to make repairs around the grounds. She was halfway up the back stairs before she had a better idea, and she called to Mr. Black, listing toward the maintenance shed under the weight of the bucket, to bring it back again.

When the going got tough, the tough got going. She was a firm believer in that proverb, she reminded herself as she brought up a handful of the nails and let them dribble back again. After all, hadn't she thought of a way for the guides to explain when black tourists first started asking about the President's slaves?

The portrait of the First Lady would be trouble, too, unless she took things in hand.

"Why, it's just awful!" Rose Cunningham cried as she joined the group in the Ladies Heritage Association Room and gazed up at the portrait propped on the mantle. "It's the ugliest, most hideous thing I've ever seen!"

The lady in the painting was enormously fat. She gazed across a century to greet the Ladies, her dignity immense, but her person equally so, and the artist had rendered both in magnificent and pitiless detail. The loose flesh hung from her cheeks and from her arms, and her long skirts partly hid a white cat at her feet but not her chubby thighs. She was plumper than any cherub who had ever flitted above an altar or peeked out from the borders of a Valentine card.

"Well, 1821, it says down here in the corner," Daisy Belle Hopkins observed. "She was dying then, you know."

"I still say it's a scandal," Rose Cunningham insisted. "I wouldn't be surprised if it were a forgery, made up by some hireling painter to embarrass the President!"

"No, ladies," Birdie Tucker said gravely. "I'm afraid it's only too genuine. M. Larry Brown says so."

Daisy Belle Hopkins teetered before the fireplace. "The poor woman," was all she could say.

"I have an idea, girls," Grace May said. "You all remember that picture we got of the President's son—summer before last, wasn't it, Birdie?—that M. Larry Brown was about to throw out. The artist's signature was forged, he said. And we got the art professor from the college to fix it. He did the trick with two little strokes"—she flicked a bracleted wrist—"even if he was so *fancy*. Couldn't we just call him in again and get him to cover up those arms, put some shadow in that neck, make her look like the lady she was? It'd be indecent to let a soul see her like this."

Flora Adams interrupted. "And do you remember, Grace dear, what Mr. Fancy Pants charged us for that ten minutes' work? Well, it was almost exactly twice what the Association has in the bank right now. Maybe we could do this. Maybe we could do that. But as treasurer of the Ladies Heritage Association, I have to insist on some practicalities. Don't forget, we still haven't paid Barney for the most recent crate of doorknobs."

That annoyed Birdie Tucker. "Mr. Black had to spend a fortune to bring in that tulip bed around the portico. We also owe Barney—even at wholesale—for that suggestion, too."

Daisy Belle was about to cry. "Oh, girls, let's not have a fuss. What the Ladies Heritage Association needs is, well—a spirit of helpfulness!"

Birdie Tucker could see that it was time to take charge.

"Well, then, the pleasure of the group. Flora?"

"We can't afford it, and that's that."

"Rose?"

"We certainly can't let anybody see her like this, either!"

"Daisy Belle?"

"Oh, I just want her to live in this house the way she really was, gracious, beautiful—"

"Grace?"

"Well, whatever the rest think. . . ."

"Then it's settled," Birdie Tucker declared. She smiled prettily and inclined her head toward Flora Adams. "And Flora, dear, Barney had been so good to extend us time, and I think I have a way to settle with him. . . ."

From behind the curtains of the President's guestroom, Birdie Tucker waited for the Legionnaires to disembark from the big tour bus and settle down. She thought that making up in those caps like soldiers was right silly. And they carried on worse than those Future Farmers had, poking at each other and snorting and grinning behind their sunglasses. Finally, Laurie managed to get their attention.

"The square of stones you see just past the large cedar tree is the original foundation of the smokehouse that served the mansion in the early 1800s. In those days the family kept a large herd of cattle and processed all the meat for its own use as well as a surplus that it sold in town. Those operations were curtailed when the President left for Washington, and the smokehouse was dismantled. The Ladies Heritage Association has made available nails from the original building at one dollar each, with proceeds going to the upkeep of these grounds. You will have an opportunity to purchase one in the gift shop at the end of our tour."

Beyond the ridge of sunlit trees that bordered the yard, the smoke from Mr. Black's fire billowed upward. Sitting in the window, Birdie Tucker could hear the spit and crackle of flames as they ravished canvas and ancient oils and lacquers.

"Now," Laurie said, "If you'll come this way, please."

CAKE AND COFFEE

Huge hot bulbs threw fingers of light along the piers of the tower, and the reflected light trembled in the fountain. The pledge class from one of the sororities had dumped in bubble bath, and the night breeze picked up bubbles and smashed them against the bronze thighs of the horses in the sculpture looming above the pool.

By pressing his face against the dirty screen of his dorm room, David could see when the music auditorium was lit at night. In warm weather when the window could be left open, bars from Joseph Hallam's playing drifted up through the sycamores on the esplanade. From then until fall the trees kept arpeggios and turns of phrase within the tower complex.

Tonight the lights burned brightly behind the narrow windows. David picked up the sheets of music from his desk and went down to the street. A car careened by, faces and bodies pressed against the cushions. He crossed to the tower, and pressed the button, and the elevator doors slithered open.

In the familiar lobby, a janitor in army fatigues was swinging a mop wide and loose in the subdued lamplight. David nodded and crossed over to the auditorium doors. Hallam sat at the keyboard, his shoulders stooped beneath the steep gable of the grand piano. He was working slowly toward a passage, the chords building upon one another toward a resolution for which the listener was made to long.

He had taught David to work methodically, patiently, and his way of entering the music, veering away from easy satisfaction and showmanship made David call him mentor. Some nights David lay awake in his warren in the vast throbbing dormitory, and played in his head the passages that he and Hallam had wrought that afternoon on the keys. He heard the notes in his head but through his fingers he felt the seamless patterns put into the music by the composer.

As he stood now watching his teacher, he remembered the night that Hallam had played the premiere of "The Depths Behind the Moon." David drew a seat next to old Fertweiler, who held the chair of modern European history and who was generally regarded as a pompous fool. At the end when the audience leaped to its feet with little cries, the old man sat still. David, applauding furiously, turned and looked down at him. His ridiculous cravat had slipped loose of his collar and splayed over his sunken chest. And he sat weeping.

David walked down the aisle that gave onto the backstage. Climbing the steps softly, he let his eyes adjust to the darkness. Cables threaded across the dirty plank floor. Out on the boards he lifted his head and followed the lines made by the seats up to rear of the house. Hallam was playing still, the notes rising tortuously, holding back the vibrant music.

David cleared his throat softly.

The hands moved on, over the keys, past another bar, and another.

"Sir?"

Hallam stopped. He shut his eyes and spun around. Then he looked hard at the boy, pinning him where he stood.

"What do you *want?*" he shouted.

David felt the blood drain from his face.

"I'm sorry, I didn't mean to bother you. I—"

"Well, you are bothering me!" Hallam leaped to his feet. The bench toppled and landed on its hard edge, with a noise like a shot through the yawning room.

David stood rigid. Colors seemed to stream from the blazing stage lights into the air. Then, trembling, he turned and stumbled into the wing. The EXIT sign over the door to the plaza gave a red cast to the cramped space. He slammed the bar and scrambled down the fire stairs to the plaza.

Just missing a stone pot that held a withering shrub, he ran, without looking, across the street.

His breath was coming in gulps when he reached the stairwell at the south end of the dormitory. The entryway stank of vomit overlain by a cleaning compound. Far above him a door opened. Laughter and running feet rattled on the stairs, then were cut off as another door slammed.

David leaned against the pocked concrete and burst into tears.

After awhile he started up the steps to the floor where he lived. No one passed him in the hall. Despite his shaking hands, the key found the lock, and he was inside, throwing the bolts behind him.

He had bought the whisky for no reason, except for the illicit fun of it because he was under age. He kept it hid, equally to no purpose, behind the towels and sweaters in the closet. His cup was stained from tea. He broke the stamps from around the neck of the bottle and poured.

The brightness from the windows was the first awareness he had. More dimly there was a rapping, receding and returning. His head throbbed, and he sank back toward sleep when the knocking came again, harder, at the door. He was wide awake. His father. The recital at home. He was on his feet instantly, slipping the bottle back into the closet. "Just a minute," he called, his voice high and reedy.

While David packed hurriedly, his father moved the truck from the head resident's parking space, where he had left it with the emergency flashers flaring. Making small talk, they drove the bitter roads of the inner city toward the interstate.

As the truck pulled off the pavement a few miles outside the city, Paul stood up from where he'd been resting in the shade of a sign.

"Open the door for him, David," his father said.

The boy pulled on the handle. Paul was ambling through the

long grass that the state had not cut since the tourist season was nearly over.

"You got to give it a real good jerk, son."

David tried again. The door squeaked and popped on dry hinges. Paul stepped up on the running board and slid inside. The smell of gas and exhaust from the highway blew in on the hot midday air.

"Hiya, slick," Paul said to David, and whistled through his front teeth. "Sharp suit. Going courtin'?"

"Tonight's my recital. That's why I'm going home this weekend." It sounded to him as though someone else's voice was speaking his words.

David's father craned his neck and looked into the rearview mirror, pressing a foot down on the accelerator. As they pulled out, the surveying rods and gear in the back shifted and settled again.

"I believe I can smell that coffee already, Mel," Paul said. He pulled the brim of his cap down on his sunburned forehead. The brown paper band was dark with sweat.

The seat of the cab sagged in the middle, and David sat low in the springs. He looked up at his father, who shifted into high gear.

"Don't worry, son. I promised your mother we'd have you there in time."

They came out onto scrub land. Daisies grew in the median, whipped by hot wind fanning across the highway. Nothing but cedars flourished on the bluffs. Now and then lovers had left their tags, like runic signs in the layered limestone. ROD LOVES CAROLINE. JF + LL

Back from the highway there were silos, gleaming in the sun and farmhouses at the ends of fields, cool and still under maple trees in the bright afternoon.

Suddenly before David's eyes was Hallam's face, bright and red as he sprang from the bench. He heard it crash again on the floor, and his shoes slapping the pavement and the breath in his head—

The truck's turn signal began to CLICK-click, CLICK-click in the dash. It slowed, David's father working it through the lower gears.

David wondered what would happen if he turned and said to him that he wanted to stop right there, and then, standing on the burning pavement, said to his father, "I don't want to be your son anymore." What if he walked across the fields to a house, in a green cove of maples, leaving the music, the college, and all the rest behind him?

Once they left the interstate the air was cooler, and the sun low enough to be eclipsed by the tallest trees. A crow flew alongside the truck for a hundred yards before veering away.

"Yonder she is," Paul said. "Hey, slick, you going to have some cake and coffee, too?"

Through the trees David saw the dull flash of a tin roof. His father turned the truck onto an unpaved road. Gravel popped from beneath the tires. Yellowwood trees grew along the clay banks. The lowest branches were covered in dust.

As they pulled into the treaded lane that ran to the back of the cabin, Paul reached over David and tapped the horn three times. The truck rolled to a stop in a low place.

A blueware pot overflowing with geraniums sat braced upright in a rotting stump. A morning glory vine had begun creeping up the iron and concrete housing above the well. The tiny trumpets were closed against the heat.

In the attic of the house there was a single window, trimmed in white, a plain, unstarched curtain drawn across it.

David studied everything except the two women who came down the steps of the back porch.

His father pulled up the handbrake and opened the door, the dust they had raised blowing past them. Paul was already hallway up the hill, leaving the cab door open behind him. David stepped down to the ground and shut it gently. Slowly he walked around to the front of the truck, giving his father time to move away.

One of the women stepped forward and kissed his father on

the mouth.

They turned in David's direction. The woman who stood beside his father waved for him to come up. David pretended it was a hello. He raised a hand vaguely and sat down on the bumper.

At his back carcasses of insects were pinned against the grill. and the manifolds of the engine clicked and cooled. After awhile the four people in the yard went inside, the screen door stretching, then swinging shut.

In the trees the dryflies screamed.

The girl came from around the front of the cabin. He watched her as she made a wide, casual circle, then disappeared. In a few minutes he heard her approaching from behind the truck.

The first notes she whistled sounded like a hymn, then fell into a lazy tunelessness. David ignored her.

A thorny pod from one of the weds that grew in the ditch flew past his face. When he did not turn around, another one hit him on the shoulder and bounced onto the hood of the truck.

"Cat got your tongue?" the girl asked.

He turned and looked at her. She sat down on the ground and stretched out her bare slender legs.

"I'm practicing," he said.

"What're you mean, 'practicing'?"

"I have a recital tonight, a piano recital." He looked in her direction, but let his eyes focus on the field behind her.

The fierce yellow light burned around her at the edge of his vision. He had noticed cockleburs clinging to her thin dress.

"There was a piano in my maw-maw's house," she said. "I seen it when we used to go visiting. I don't know what became of it when her things was sold. Couldn't none of us play, so we let it go."

David wanted to be out on the highway again.

"I kind of wish now we'd of kept that piano," she said. "I bet you play real good."

Hues leaped out of the white light that burned around them, as though they stood at the entrance to a stage. At the edge of a far field, a buzzard rose flapping from a dark tree and wheeled away from the farm over the sunlit surface of the mountain.

"Hey," the girl said, getting to her feet and taking two steps toward him. "You want to go up to the house with me?"

Before he thought, David was on his feet, standing in the dust and shouting at her. "No! I don't want to go up to the house with you! Can't you see that I despise you? Why don't you leave me alone?"

She fell back as if he had hit her across the face.

"You're crazy!" she said. "I think you must be crazy."

David felt the sweat trickle down his back. His breath came fast and the blood pulsed in his neck.

The girl stood where she was, rocking for a moment on her bare feet. Her small brown eyes narrowed, and her mouth turned down at the corners. Then she turned with a jerk and started back toward the cabin with a determined lope.

The illumined world seemed to expand before David. He looked up toward the bald on the mountain. He longed to climb to it, over the hot pine needles and around the tepid pools hid in the undergrowth into that bright field. From there he would almost be able to touch the sky.

He turned back to watch the girl as she went up the steps, making a curious little half-turn on each one, toward the door into the cabin. She pulled open the screen, halted, and looked back toward David standing in the road. She flung open the screen door and stepped inside, letting it slam behind her.

A GIFT OF CHARITY

"The Queen is coming," I said.

The purr of the oxygen tank was the only sound in the room.

"The Queen?" rasped Mary Frances Alexander.

"To dedicate the new east front. I thought I'd told you."

I had told her, of course, twice before. But we kept up the fiction of her full presence of mind.

"For shame," she said, and grinned a nearly cadaverous grin. "How can I be a Friend of the Cathedral if you keep secrets from me?"

"But I haven't, Mrs. Alexander. You really are one of the first to know. There's been nothing in the papers."

"No, that's true." She let her head sink back into the pillows.

My hat was on the table by the water pitcher. As I reached for it, my hand obscured the room reflected in its silver surface.

"No, please stay," she implored. "Although you must have other duties, other Friends—"

I did, but it was not important. "Mrs. Alexander is potentially our largest benefactor, Father Jonathan," the bishop himself had said to me. "I trust you'll see that she doesn't want for anything."

Lucky Jim, we called him, when he first came to us from Charleston, which had always been closer to Canterbury than even Boston was. Of his old friend from undergraduate days, Mrs. Alexander, he meant simply: the spiritual offices, a volunteer from the Guild to read to her, and my constant attention.

How many years had it been since he'd given me that commission? Could it be nearly ten?

Ten years. Millions of heartbeats. Many thousands of breaths of air. And endless masses strummed or chanted, as the fashion changed over the decade that had begun with whale songs in the antiphony and closed with recessionals of imperial theme.

The interview between Lucky Jim and me had taken place not long after St. Peter, presiding on the apex of the east front, pitched forward and shattered to pieces on the steps. "Vandals again!" thought our brother Donald, when he found the rubble during his morning run around the close. He was on retreat among us, being, in the life that ours often parodied, a state senator from West Hartford with ambitions for Congress.

But no angel was gone from among the lower orders, which rose as high as a street juvenile could throw a rock. By the time the police arrived, the fog had burned away from the face. Donald rode with them out to the east parking lot to show them the access road that he surmised had been entered during the night. From there they could see the *sede vacante*, not many feet below the Coptic cross and its lightning rod.

I gave them coffee and croissants and apologized for the trouble we'd put them to. "Forget it, Father," said the one with the walrus mustache. "Happens all the time."

The following Thursday the structural engineers showed up during the 7:30 a.m. service where I was officiating. By the time I had distributed communion, they were balanced on their pulley, working their way upward. Along the way they paused occasionally to trace a line of mortar laid a century before by a laborer whose bones were moldering in a potters field. An hour later they descended like avenging angels.

"It's every bit going to have to come down," said the senior man, shifting his hard hat from hand to hand as we sat in Lucky Jim's study. "Else in a really bad storm, the whole blessed thing— Sorry, bishop, just a manner of speaking."

"That's all right, Mr. Sloan," Jim said. He was reared back in his episcopate swivel chair. "I trust you spoke rightly. And the Lord only knows where we'll get the money."

"It's the air," the engineer went on. "From the beltway. And the industry that's gone in. You can break pieces off in your hand, up there on that face."

Standing at the back of the room, I slipped out, so if the bishop had an answer, I did not hear it. No one saw me leave.

In my own, simpler quarters, I drew out of an envelope the estimates I'd just received for new cushions under the communion rail. The party—stalwart engineers and anxious, poised bishop, moved past my door, onto the cloisters, and toward the panel truck shimmering in the heat. The papers shuffled through my fingers and slithered down the sides of the wastebasket.

"What if we asked 5,000 well-to-do communicants across the country to give $1,000 each?" our brother Harvey asked. "You know, 'a national drive for the national shrine.'"

"Why not approach five of the top ones to give a million?" said Owen (who behind his back we called "the Jesuit" for his passionate peevishness). "I've heard a million's nothing nowadays."

Our brother Rhodes had been called to the chair. The only rule governing this session on the future of the cathedral, he announced, was that there would be none. We should assume the feasibility of any idea. One or two of high church persuasion fidgeted.

"Well, there's always bingo," noted Joel, who was our clown but also the best Old Testament man among us. Father Rhodes admonished the assembly for the general groan, but hurried on.

The ideas flew on extended wings to the outer limits of civility, common sense, what honest churchmen could do: Selling pews. Holding lotteries. Going chiefly to designer labels at the thrift shop.

"We could sow winter wheat on those north grounds. Only, with the beltway passing over it, we'd probably lose our crop to a cigarette fire, sooner or later." This from Franklin, who had been born in the imaginary country of North Dakota.

"Remember, Father," admonished Rhodes from the chair. "No qualifications." He wrote down the idea on his legal pad. We compiled another page and were approaching simony when I spoke up.

"Might we mention the, ah, indebtedness just before every offertory?" No one demurred.

As it happened I served at the Eucharist in St. John of Arimithea the next Sunday. There was standing room only, since our bus picked up at the condominiums along Sterling Avenue for that service. When I explained the Cathedral's plight, an intake of breath was heard in the room. The wicker plate followed quickly. Later, as I brought down the consecrated host, I glanced out of the corner of my eye at the sheaf of bills, spilling over each other like slapstick actors.

We impressed into our team an accountant from the congregation, who reviewed the tax status of our various enterprises (and who couldn't resist a predictable little joke about "rendering unto Caesar.") In time we accumulated a small portfolio of stocks in companies that did not discriminate, make armaments, or have anything to do with tobacco. Our brother Isadore, having a Wharton M.B.A., dealt with the broker.

At Izzy's suggestion, we asked for an increase in our annual stipend, set by Congress, for the care of the Revolutionary War graveyard on our grounds. We also made it known that the Cathedral was available for weddings of socialites' sons and daughters, and thereby acquired several donations.

To two new parishes of dissenting Catholics, we rented out chapels. One group intimated how sorry they were that the Church continued officially to call us heretics. The other asked mildly if we would object to a rite of purification.

As an economy measure we shut off the light inside the dome during the day. The murals disappeared into the blackness.

At the next retreat after the engineers' disclosure, the bishop's seminar on "Gifts" followed mine on "New Attitudes Toward Grieving." "We're going to become aggressive, moving-out servants of God," Lucky Jim declared. He proceeded to describe the differences between outright and contingency bequests, and among annuities, unitrusts, and remainder trusts. His talk raised the Scholastics to a new level of appreciation in my mind.

"Ah, Father Jonathan," the Bishop greeted me afterward, when his hand and mine accidentally reached for the same slice of brie on toast at the same moment. I looked up from the episcopal ring into the beaming face.

He took the hors d'oeuvre. "I *thought* the sun suddenly seemed brighter, the air sweeter—"

"And how about the cream?" I asked clasping his hand. "Less low-level radiation?"

"Ah, the cynicism of youth! But you're all of you too quick for an old man like me. Do you realize I was born during FDR's first administration? But then again, how could that be of any interest to you?"

As with most monumentally vain men, his self-effacement could be perfectly disarming. Before I knew it, he was walking us, arm around my shoulder, away from the crowd.

"Now, Father, there's a matter I've meant to get your judgment on for some time. A question of public relations, I guess you'd say. The scaffolding may be up around the east front for awhile. We'll hear grumbling, I know, from the tourist people and maybe our parishioners, too. What should I say?"

It was impossible not to admire the old reprobate, who sat on national commissions by appointments of presidents and who would sell the chalice if it came to that. I chose the wrong moment not to take him seriously. In humor, as in extreme unction, timing could be everything.

"Not my area, I'm afraid," said I. "Apologetics. Augustine. Terminal counseling."

"Why, yes, of course," he said expansively. "My goodness, Father, why I know what you've meant to our little band over the years." He turned until we were face to face, towering above me. I remembered that he had lettered in basketball at Clemson, from which distinction many had gone on to make money, few to become bishops of the Church, and fewer still to do both.

The wing where we were standing was used to store the penitential vestments for Lent, and it could be unimaginably forlorn of an afternoon. The atmosphere made Jim's tone even weightier.

"Father, I have a very special task for you. Will you do it?" The question was purely for form.

By the time we reached the close, the pigeons were nesting near the downspouts. Chimes from speakers in the bell tower, mixed by one of the sound studios in town, pealed down the hill toward the rush hour traffic.

"So you see, Father Jonathan, Mrs. Alexander and I go back some way." He clapped a hand against each shoulder and grinned, then strode away waving. "Get to know her, will you. And let me know how things progress."

On my first visit, and for several years thereafter, Mary Frances Alexander held forth from a wingback chair. Her original and abiding subject was her Admiral, who had built the estate that surrounded us. She kept the anniversary of his death in mourning and prayed to the patron saint of sailors that he might be admitted to the regions of light where she could in time rejoin him. Meanwhile she chaired the foundation that bore his name.

Sometimes our conversation moved on to other subjects, such as how she had cured herself of primary anemia by eating massive amounts of peanut butter. And there were tales of Palm Springs a generation before. These she plainly bowdlerized out of respect for my office, leaving the details to my all too fertile imagination.

"Is it true," I once ventured, "that you and Lucky—uh, the Bishop had a profitable business at Clemson supplying—well, I find this awkward, now that I've begun—as middlemen between a certain backwoods manufacturer and the fraternities?"

She straightened, and the image of our tumbling facade flashed before my eyes. "'Awkward?'" she exploded into laughter. "Why should it be? Why, we were young and enterprising. And we were a local legend. Now, here's the way it came about—"

Her story went on for a full hour without pause. During it, a cat crept out of some lair and sailed without warning into my lap.

It shifted, settled, then raised its lantern eyes full upon me. I was attentive to the creature, even though it caused a skin rash, and thereafter remembered to send Mrs. Alexander cat books that I spotted at remainder sales. And at the Bishop's Council, which we created for our most promising prospects and which counseled nothing, I never failed to ask about "Wee-Gee," the loathsome creature's name.

Whenever I could I opened a conversation on the subject that had brought me to her. After the fourth year of my visits began, I carried in my satchel, along with my prayer book, the unsigned codicil to her will that would make the Cathedral her legatee.

"Perpetuating your stewardship" was one of my euphemisms. She would not hear it, or any other that I could devise. "There's plenty of time, Father Jonathan. There's a dance or two in this old dame yet."

It occurred to me that her delay had a purpose, which was to extend my visits indefinitely. I should continue to come and listen for as long as it took her to die.

The stonecutters sat up their yard next to the Cathedral, and the diamond teeth of their saws sang, followed by the thonk-thonk-thonk of their chisels. We numbered and sold the stones, inscribing each purchaser's name in a Golden Book of Remembrance. That and our luncheons for the political and financial power elite of the city paid the rig haulers who brought the massive rocks up from the quarries of Tennessee.

Take the long view, the clerk of the works advised Jim. It was easy for him to say, over sherry and biscuits in the immaculate kitchen kept by the parish ladies. It was me, waiting at Mrs. Alexander's side, who had to wait until the right words concerning her will were breathed into me.

Her crippling came suddenly, in its swiftness a blessing, though not one recognized in our rite. In November before her 79th birthday, she took up a cane. By spring her garden wall inscribed the only world in which she could move about with certainty. She instructed the yard man to set traps that would stop moles from building tunnels that might trip her, and she shuffled over the Admiral's land for as long as she could.

When the bones in her feet gave way, her hands too became less steady. In time her dresses seemed to hang on her increasingly stolid and ungainly frame. The loss of elegance was to her the first serious disability and made her take more and more to her bed.

From there she talked on, after I finished reading to her, about the world she remembered, which would one day be as dim as the one that built the first cathedrals. It, too, would leave only mysterious traces.

Mrs. Alexander would gracefully tell me when each visit was over. There being no touch from my hand that seemed exactly fitting, I would let myself out.

That is how I imagined it would be when she died. Someone would telephone us, and I would report the news, along with the failure or my object, to Jim. Yet, truthfully, as the new east front of the Cathedral began to rise, I gave less thought to these last things. Mary Frances Alexander resisted the silence with voice and memory, and they were declarations for life. Due to some peculiar failure of eyesight, she had to look at the ceiling to see me clearly, but even with that peripheral gaze she held me steadily, and at her pleasure.

Who, indeed, I realized would repossess an archangel to satisfy some account past due?

When Buckingham Palace announced the Queen's American visit, our brother Geoffrey, who occasionally published poetry in little magazines, suggested we invite her to dedicate our undertaking. Lucky Jim asked me to handle it, and I told Her Majesty's representative that we would try to have the scaffolding removed for the occasion.

MONTAGE

The last love of my youth became an historian of Soviet silent film, recently achieving tenure at her university, while I took over the city's oldest unsolved murder case with no prospects for finding the answers.

I had you every other weekend that summer of 1971, in your parents' home, across the river from Louisville. I'd arrive, greeted by a nuzzle from your old, smelly dog, Yoki, a drink from your father, and an hour of sex play in the den, where we were allowed to go and close the door.

"Before you get here, Mom always asks me, 'Are you coordinated?'" you told me, meaning did the colors of your outerwear and your underwear match.

"Well, are you?" I teased. And you showed me.

We went to harness races, and Stephen Foster's home, where "Jeannie With the Light Brown Hair" wafted softly from a hi-fi speaker, and parked in the hills that looked down on the Falls of the Ohio. You could reel off the English succession, through revolutions and scandal. I, who had helped bring down a president over Viet Nam, was beguiled by this.

"My parents have no philosophy," you warned me, who was at the time a divinity school student. "Mom says I should look for a good provider."

Without saying it, youasked only that I declare for a direction and a place in the world: America, a good job, buying power, and you would entwine those glorious legs around me every night. When I did not you married S., won a Ph.D. at Stanford, and published your tenure-winning book on cinema as Gorbachev fell and Tower began offering Eisenstein in its foreign section.

The Quentin case came to me in a bulging accordion file. Labels had flaked from folders. Old thermofax paper was hardened. The lawyer's bludgeon slaying had been for years an embarrassment, because the department made it a point of pride that no murder case would ever be closed, even if could, at the same time, never be solved.

Who was Quentin to me? No one I'd ever know, but an obsession all the same. It seemed to me that I'd been an eyewitness, standing by happenstance in the trees by the park when he'd been set upon and his head beaten in by two men who, having planned the crime, ran for their car and pealed out, leaving tread marks on the asphalt.

The earliest theory, that spring of 1953, was that he'd been leading a double life, married to Mary Jane Ireland Quentin but with a girl attending Vanderbilt, whose jealous boyfriend and a confederate solved the problem in a tidy way. The picture of Mary Jane, with her Japanese sumo-wrestler's body, lent a certain plausibility to this interpretation.

Retired sergeant Pritchard, who'd done the legwork on this angle, I interviewed in the nursing home. There were questions you couldn't ask back then, he said. At the young woman's sorority house, he even had the door shut in his face. Two days later the chief of detectives had dropped by, seemingly just passing down the hall, straddled the straightback chair with his chest to the back, and allowed that he thought another line of inquiry might get further.

You and S. are now America's longest-married couple of yourage, marking a quarter-century together in yourmid-forties. Over the years I have imagined yourerotic life with this man, with whom you grew up and came into your vocation. I never met him, haven't an inkling what he looks like, nor who he is, nor what he does for a living, although I have followed you, figuratively speaking, across the continent. There's a craft in my work, although little daring. If I had been daring I would have married you before S. ever saw you.

I assume the story of your love, any love, if told to the full, would make a book. There would be chapters on hours of making love. On remaking the bond after quarrels that might have ended it. On peaceful, passionate intensity. You had gone to California with him in your early years, and facing middle age, you returned east for your tenure track job, he risking whatever stake he'd had out there. Why his secrecy? Why is he in no directory, no phone book, no police record anywhere?

The Quentin case remained for years a silent curse over the city. Certain friends quietly stopped speaking, certain names were expunged from invitation lists, three families actually left town. Briefly, Quentin's law partner was a suspect, although he had nothing to do with it, he lost his seat in the legislature. I saw him a few weeks ago, a withered old man, in traffic court. The murderers took one life, the papers this other.

What have I to go on? On Friday afternoons, in making out my weekly report, I heft and spread out the files across my desk like cards in a game of solitaire. Here is the cat-and-mouse interview with Mrs. Jameson, a first cousin of Quentin, a second cousin of the publisher of the afternoon paper, who told her to carry the secret to her grave. If she knew the identity of the murderers she played with me like a coquette, stringing it out into a series of lunches, "Well, now, I've heard that name. Let me think. . . " and I ordered her another sherry.

And there's a strange letter from Judge T. Weir Phillips to his friend Mrs. Bowdouin of Sewanee, about a fraudulent land deal that Quentin was going to expose to the federal attorney. J. Edgar Hoover had declined one of my predecessors' requests for FBI files in the case.

What have I to go on why you left me? You hated school, chaffed under life in your parents' home that summer. I who had never had a woman hesitated. But S. offered you California, and with him you found your love and your work. Solshenitsyn the holy man of Russia took up residence in Vermont, and you and S. followed, as if magical lines of light touch on the planet by your mind, by the lantern light, by projectors flickering in the dark theater. You, I assume, believe that all those footnotes about movies for the masses, in Roman and Cyrillic, matter across time.

From the water sluicing down the drainpipe outside my apartment, I understand how even the sibilance of water could mask the plan of conspirators. The soughing of the wind covers the sound of a skull shattering. The ambient roar of the interstate beyond my balcony washes the city like a sea wave, carrying off a club, a gun, a shiv.

The world sometimes wraps murder in profound silence. Whenever I go to the City Club as a guest, old men who might or might not have been involved avert their eyes from me as they saw their roast beef with spotted hands. My files I have divided into two stacks, that which seems to corroborate two men as the killers, and that which leads out into the hall of mirrors. In the former was investigating officers notes about footprints. In the latter were secret checkups on Quentin's colleague at the bar who had named a son for one of the authors of the land deal.

Do you dream in Russian? Do you tease S. with Russian words when you play in bed, and clasp him in words of history and revolution and shafts of light to the screen? Is your marriage the history of that land from Napoleon to the great patriotic war to Krushchev's saber-rattling while watching the May Day parades of missles? Did your perfect love and faith-keeping with America tear down the stones of the Lubyanka?

I have tried to imagine what it is like to think in another language, but having failed in words of my own to you. . . .

Your vocation came at last into the world commercial culture. I typed a label for the notes I made from old Pritchard, and slipped them into the front of the current folder.

You called it second sight, that inheritance from your *grandmere*, and that you would have turned back if you could have. Instead, you had no choice but to look into my future, and you learned that I had no calling, would never find a place in the world. You called yourself a Nietschzean, and you understood that the only lives for rebels was in the academy or in alienation. So you pursued the professorate. There are a dozen people in the world, here and in Russia, who know what you know. They are your community, they read your books, you theirs. But how different is your work from mine, really? You, like me, have only the sources that survive. You wrap interpretation around this detritus and call it history. All I have are scraps of paper, without coherence, for a grand jury that will never sit.

Mine is the besetting sin in America, a lack of ambition, of middle-class striving. "Find a good provider," your mother told you, and your father said, "I'm glad R's going to graduate school. He's not cut out for business." Later, after your wedding, he wrote to me to tell me, and to say, gently, "Live your life." As for the life I have lived, I will never close the Quentin case. Forever will you love and, forever, in these files is terror without end.

SOLSTICE

The fall that Charles Woods, just before he lost his job, fell in love, briefly, for the last time.

The girl had been sitting at a bar in the Tulane Hotel, talking earnestly with another woman. He supposed they worked together at the Hospital Alliance Corporation or Trans-Pacific Cellular, but It occurred to him later, as he thought about their clothes that perhaps they were dressed to see a play at the performing arts center

He'd deposited his severance paycheck and kept a little cash. He handed the waiter a ten dollar bill and his card, and asked to hand it to her with a glass of whatever she was drinking

The delivered it to the second woman, the companion of the beguiling one.

The next week his boss, going through a bloody divorce, told Woods not to return to the office. He never knew if the girl called, or how he could explain that he'd wanted to meet her friend.

Now, parking his car and zipping his parka against the wind off the river, he walked the four blocks to the bar where she had been, those months before. He assumed they did not want him there. He was older than the crowd, obviously not prosperous, alone, with thinning hair.

The loss of the job had mattered less than the failure to find the girl. He told friends that he was starting a new book, doing some consulting, involved in publishing projects, hence the days in the library. But now as he passed an hour seated by himself at a table for two, he realized how foolish he'd been to expect an old-line organization to change its ways. The company was what it wished to be, and its directors smugly proud, believing their publicity departments own promotions and the fabrications of the annual report.

It seemed to him that he had reached an impasse with the world of occupations He could not carry around his resume once again. The world had established universities for places like him, people with rough edges, honorably unfitted for the struggle of life. But he had no calling to teach.

A silver tinsel rope had been draped over the mirror above the bar and red bows and ribbons big as car doors hung from the wood pediments. In the restaurant, the pianist was playing rink-a-tink carols. It had not been asking too much of life, he thought: one task to do, one person to love. Or evidently, it had been.

He paid his tab and walked back to his car, parked at the unlit lot with a cheap all-day rate. On the inner loop traffic was backed up at the exit to the mall.

His apartment was toward the rear of the complex, away from the streetlights and the waning moon in the east reflected off the sliding glass door. The switch just inside lighted the lamp by his reading table.

Taking note of the library's closing for four holidays, he had brought home Jack London' s collected stories, which he had not read in graduate school. He stopped in the hall to turn up the thermostat, then went to the kitchen and put his dinner in the oven.

The weather girl spoke of temperatures dropping overnight. It was the first night of winter.

He sat down to wait for the timer on the stove. The wine was still warm in his veins. It was well, he thought, not to believe or hope in things that had not been and would now not ever be.

From his pile of books, he picked one, but then in a few pages lost the thread and realized there was a distraction in the room. At the unit across the parking lot, old Mr. Thurston, the retired civil servant, had put up his crèche and wise men on the little margin of brown grass by the pavement. The star over the little ceramic figures was flashing, whether from some shortage in the wire or novelty of the manufacturer. Charles sat down his book, walked across the room, and drew the curtains.

Across town, in the upstairs bedroom of a restored Queen Anne house, the girl with curly brown hair and eyes made of stars let fall her terry cloth robe in a gesture without thought that would have taken Charles's breath away. She snapped off the light, pulled up the quilt around her, and cried herself to sleep. Shortly after two a.m., the great north half of the earth began ever so slightly to cant in its orbit.

WITH KENNEDY

I'd dealt Steve and me three cards apiece when the next one going to him stuck to my fingertips and fell face side up. A two of clubs. I had to reshuffle and start over. I lost the hand when Steve came up with a flush. He scraped the pot of nickels and dimes over to his side of the table.

San Antonio in November can be like August back home in Tennessee. We were in our undershirts, soaking up a meager breeze from a revolving tabletop fan. The windows were up, and we could hear an occasional 'Ten HUT' and a snap of an M-1 bolt from the parade ground.

Still, I was just as glad to be at Lackland instead of back at the Pentagon, or shipping out to Nam as some of my old Washington buddies were, they figuring it was the best way up the ladder. Just not ambitious enough for this man's Air Force, I guess.

Steve was clacking the cards through his hands for his deal when we heard footsteps along the porch. Major Earles opened the door. That was another nice thing about this post: the brass didn't expect a salute unless there were superior officers around.

The major made a little joke about the size of the pot and how it was a good thing the paymaster wasn't handing out divvy. We laughed, then he got down to business. "Okay, fellows, listen up now. It's dress blues tomorrow. Some of the unit's going to be escorting the President's car and directing traffic at the speaking. I want you two to sit on the platform."

We shot the bull for awhile longer. Earles was a lifer, just a kid when he'd joined up, been wounded in Korea. He was one of the few who'd be wearing a combat ribbon next day.

Steve and I rode over to the ball field that Thursday in his '61

'Vette, which he'd shined up for the occasion, till the red paint job was so bright it hurt your eyes. He loved that car better than anything, and that's why our penny-ante game. He spent every dime he had buying new gizmos for it.

He parked on the grass way out at the edge of the park and a good walk from the bleachers. "We can beat the traffic getting out," he said. He was off duty next day, and ready to start his three-day weekend. The car got him a lot of babes, I knew that much.

Buses were lined up along the main road in, one with a banner that read "Democratic Women's Club Welcomes JFK." Kids in band uniforms were climbing out of one of the yellow schoolbuses. A short fat boy was tuning up his tuba, wrenching notes out of the horn, a sound like cows in a rut. On the way in to the platform, we walked by a troupe of cowgirls, and I spotted a cute one checking her makeup in her compact.

A plywood platform had been cobbled together, about twenty yards out from the front row of the bleachers. Officers and wives got the folding chairs that'd been set up in between the two. The bleachers were for civilians from San Antone and around about, and the seats were almost all taken. Some of the ladies wore "Kennedy / Johnson '64" buttons by their boutonnieres, which were wilting in the heat.

I gave a wave to my buddy Barney Brooks, sitting in the officer's section, who answered with a 'Hey, look at you!' nod and grin. He'd co-piloted the chopper on the last Mercury pickup.

Finally the presidential party filed on. Kennedy was taller than I'd thought. He managed to smile through what must have been the umpteenth rendition of "The Eyes of Texas Are Upon You" that he'd heard. The wife of the base commandant waddled to the podium to announce that the First Lady would not be on hand as she had gone back to her hotel to rest. There was a titter of disappointment among the Democratic women. Then, his chestful of medals thrust out, the general himself introduced our guest.

The clipped New England speech sounded from the conical

loudspeakers over the dry, dusty fields, which seemed to absorb the words like rain. The President said something about "the perils facing liberty" and "the challenges to the free world" and "the men and women of the United States Air Force, ready to sacrifice. . . ." I didn't keep up with politics, but I knew he was here to settle some party squabble, and this wasn't a big part of the trip or anything. I felt sort of sorry for the guy, everybody wanting a piece of him.

The flashbulbs popped, and the crowd clapped whenever Kennedy paused after the speechwriter's good lines. He talked for maybe fifteen minutes, and by the time he finished there was a little breeze. The crepe paper draping the platform fluttered and clattered.

Protocol said we were to stay till the President and his party had left, but Steve and I figured that if we stuck around, some officer would find something for us to do, just to make himself look important. So we slipped out while Kennedy was flicking a pen across scraps of paper being thrust at him. I happened to catch the eye of the cute cowgirl, gripping her ballpoint and a little autograph book. This time I smiled. I might as well have been invisible.

We walked out past the presidential limousine drawn up at the side of the stage, kind of kitty-cornered, and started on a roundabout way back to the car. As we crossed the field by the ballpark, grasshoppers sprang up out of the way of our spit-shined shoes. I could hear the buses starting. A few cars were leaving the grounds, white gravel dust swirling behind them.

"Well, what say we go fox hunting tonight?" Steve asked. He meant did I want to go with him down to the strip and see if we could find some accommodating ladies.

Damn, I wanted to. We'd have something to talk about, being with Kennedy that day, and all. And it'd been a long time since that date with the theater major at Trinity, who'd said she loved uniforms but wondered what I was like without mine on.

We finally got back to the where the car was parked. I dropped to my knees to pick some burs off my cuffs, and out of habit, swipe the dust off my shoes. Steve had taken off his coat and dropped it in the back seat. He turned back to where I was, his back to the car. "Well, whadda you say?"

A couple of the burs were really sticking to the cloth and I had to use both hands, one to hold the pants leg, the other to yank.

"Look, Steve, I'd like to, I really would. But I got to come back in here tomorrow. I don't know, Earles'll probably have me over here on the cleanup detail. But anyhow, I've got that batch of damn reports that've got to get done in the next week. How late you figuring on staying out?"

When there wasn't any answer, I looked up, squinting into the sky. Steve was peering into the middle distance, with a fixed stare. I couldn't make out his expression, maybe a little startled. I stood up.

"It's Kennedy," he said, swallowing hard. And I turned around.

He was walking toward us, wearing sunglasses now, with a friendly easy grin on his face, different from his platform smile. When he was within ten feet of us, we snapped to attention and saluted our commander-in-chief.

"At ease, gentlemen." His voice was softer now, a little jaunty, too. He put out his hand to me.

"Jack Kennedy. Is this your car?"

"Sergeant-Major Anthony A. Roberts, Nashville, Tennessee, sir. No, sir, it's my buddy's here."

Kennedy walked over and shook Steve's hand, who had recovered a bit and managed to get his name and rank right. His dad had been career Air Force, so Steve wasn't from anywhere.

Kennedy walked up to the driver's side of the 'Vette, stood by the hood, and look down the side, along the lines of the body. The westering sun was in his face now.

There was something panther-like in his step. I couldn't tell you what, but Maureen, my ex-wife, probably could have, in words I hadn't known women knew. And I'd heard the stories, back in Washington, from buddies on executive office detail.

"I was just thinking, as I was walking over to you fellows, about the first time I came out here, in the spring of '36," he said, "and about that old Chevrolet of Lem Billings, my pal from Choate. We drove from Fort Worth out to Arizona in it. Stayed on a ranch, where both of us got lice. I've never liked Arizona since. Even less since it looks like Goldwater's going to try to beat me next year."

He grinned. "I split all the speeding tickets with Billings. Ever get a ticket in this car, sergeant?"

"No, sir. . .er, yes, sir," Steve managed to get out. "But never on the base, sir."

Kennedy threw back his head and laughed.

"When Dad heard about those tickets, I thought he was going to disinherit me. He didn't, but he never bought me a car like this, either. I always wanted one. Never got it."

The grin stayed in place. He asked where we'd served and about families. Kennedy nodded a little at the answers, but his eyes kept studying the chassis. Finally I thought we ought to hold up our end of the conversation.

I asked, "Are you staying on the base tonight, sir?"

"No, Mrs. Kennedy and I will be at the Hilton in town. We're leaving in the morning to go to Dallas. I've got to give another speech over there tomorrow afternoon."

There was some more small talk that soon played out. Then Kennedy actually caressed the hood of the 'Vette, as if it were flesh. "Damn great-looking wheels!" he said, and the grin flashed again.

With that he shook hands with both of us and turned away, a man surrounded by people, who'd made love with Marilyn Monroe, and who coveted my buddy's car.

We watched him all the way back across the field, relaxed and done for the day, his hand in his coat pocket. And I realized how he was all alone under that vast Texas sky.

Edwards Brothers Malloy
Thorofare, NJ USA
October 8, 2013